WALTZING in VIENNA

WALTZING in VIENNA

CG METTS

Catmoon Media
Columbia, South Carolina, USA

Catmoon Media Publishing
Columbia, South Carolina, USA
catmoon-media@mindspring.com

Edition No. 1
January 21, 2016
ISBN-13: 978-0-692-53334-5
ISBN-10: 0692533346

For Colleen
For Love— Forever

CONTENTS

ACKNOWLEDGMENTS

While writing a novel may seem like a solitary endeavor, it is actually an effort that requires many people. Some serve as muses and inspiration, others for more practical reasons, but at the heart of any real endeavor is family. So I want to thank Colleen and our sons Dashiell and Desmond for their undying support and love. Special thanks goes out to Gunner Sergeant Hensley at the Citadel. Finally, thanks to all of those friends and acquaintances who over the years, have provided a wealth of inspiration, good and bad examples of living life, humor, friendship, knowledge, and sparks that light up the imagination.

CGM

DIANA THE HUNTRESS

Awoman can always tell when a man wants her, but a man never knows if she truly desires him. The misunderstanding that he is the one in control and not her demonstrates the folly of a man, who in his desires is willing to do just about anything to have her. As she watched the real estate agent trying to pry open the door with a long screwdriver, she remembered a line from H. L. Mencken: "Temptation is a woman's weapon." Temptation was a weapon she wielded often and very accurately.

During the past few days, he had dropped thinly veiled propositions to her. They had been minor things, of course, flirtatiously looking into her eyes, saying how much he loved a woman wearing a sweater, and casually touching her shoulder when he opened the door for her.

Today he had upped his game. When she arrived in the parking lot, he took her hand, helped her out of the car, and told her with a slow drawl how beautiful she looked. The seller had given him the wrong key and now he set out to prove himself a man of action, a handyman, and a real estate agent extraordinaire. His thick band of gold flickered in the bright morning sun as he tried to work the door open. Like many men, he often kept his left hand in his pocket, but he needed two hands today.

She lit up a cigarette and took a drag. It was the first of the day, and when the pale lipstick-stained cigarette slipped out of her mouth, she let the smoke billow out. Her warm breath was made cloudy on this cold January day. The cold surprised Diana, since she had attended the College of Charleston and remembered the temperate weather. It was icy back home in Nashville, but she'd always thought of Charleston as tropical in nature, with its mix of palm trees and majestic palmettos.

Her long chestnut-colored hair fell across her shoulders, flowing from beneath a gray knit hat her sister-in-law had given her three Christmases ago. She regularly wore her hair down because she liked the way it felt as it caressed her face. It was her face that people remembered, not because she was a striking beauty, but because it was in perfect proportion. With just one look from her cool blue eyes, she had a charm that most men, and women, found hard to resist.

Wrapped around her body was a soft olive-colored sweater that felt warm against her skin. She had picked it up while on vacation in Ireland after her suitcase was lost at the airport. For the whole eight days she was there, she had lived in that sweater and the few things she had purchased at the airport gift shop. Denim was her fabric of choice and her well-worn blue jeans hugged her hips. She was neither rail-thin nor plump, her figure was unswerving since college, and she could still fit into the same clothing she had worn over the past two decades, including her most favorite article of clothing, her old deep-blue pea coat. She had bought it when she moved from Charleston to Nashville. It still fit her and hid the fact that she was now forty-two years old, as much as it hid her from the cold weather.

For her, every piece of clothing had a story, tied to stories about her past experiences and travels. Her look was direct, classic, and comfortable, much like the way she lived her life.

"Diana. I got it open."

The real estate agent had struggled with the door to the old warehouse for fifteen minutes in pure frustration, but now he looked triumphant. Diana was relieved. She flicked her cigarette to the pavement and walked over to him.

His name was Carter, and he was typically Southern in his crisp khaki pants and the salmon-colored dress shirt layered beneath his navy blue blazer and wool topcoat. His brown hair was short, and she could see the nape of his neck just above his collar. It was rough and reddish, chafed by the cold wind.

He said, "Ladies first," with old Southern charm.

When she passed him, she could smell his cologne. It was a scent she had smelled before, but she could not place the name. It was something musky, something that smelled warm on this cold day. He filed in right behind her, in a hurry to get into the building and out of the cold. His hand found a light switch and snapped it to the on position, and the hanging fluorescents flickered and came on one by one as she got her first good sight of the interior of the warehouse.

At first Diana noticed the smell of a very old building, one that had held cotton during the old days of the South, and later everything from cornmeal and flour to machine parts. Abandoned and forgotten a long time ago, the old building was now alive and newly renovated. The big open space had smooth concrete floors and plenty of windows lining the walls just below the ceiling, letting in plenty of light no matter the time of day.

"We finally got it zoned light industrial," he said. "About a year and a half ago, the owner added insulation to the walls and dropped the ceiling. He put in high-efficiency air units, and poured a new floor with electrical outlets and conduit."

He paused for a moment and smiled at her.

"He was ready to go until the city took forever to change the zoning and his business partner walked. He's motivated to sell. There are three offices and two restrooms over there on the left."

Diana looked around and smiled back at him.

"This suits our needs very well. I like the open space. Our existing facility is a bit like a maze."

She inhaled slowly.

"You think he might consider a million and a half for the place?"

"Yes, ma'am, it's worth a shot, and he'll likely counter. He lowered it to a million eight three months ago. But he's never had a serious offer on the place, so you never know."

"So far I like it. Let's go look at the offices."

He nodded okay and the two walked to the left. She let him lead and watched him walk in front of her. He had a youthful stride. It was self-assured, like that of an animal approaching its prey, for he was confident that she was ready to make an offer. It was the sixth property they had seen over the past four days, and the first she had instantly thought perfect for her needs.

The front office was more of a reception area, about the size of a small bedroom, with a large plate-glass window that overlooked the open area of the building. From here she could see everything. From the ceiling of the office, incandescent fixtures flooded down warm golden light, in contrast to the fuzzy fluorescent light in the rest of the building. Adding to the brightness of the room, the walls were clean and painted a soft cream color. A large ancient wooden desk dominated the space, covered by a stack of blueprints and assorted paperwork that had been used for the renovations. There was no chair, but Diana noticed the scuffs and scrapes where the chair had once been, the tracks where a chair and its occupant had moved in and out from this worn but solid desk. It had character, like her.

"Here, let me show you the floor plan so you can get an idea of the area and where the conduit and electrical are located."

Carter thumbed through the stack and turned over the top layer of plans.

"The inside measurements are shown here and here."

He pointed to the notations on the plans with his long sturdy finger.

Diana leaned over, next to him, looking down at the plans.

"I think this will be plenty of room, but I'd like to

get a copy of the plans to our shop manager back home. We have several textile presses, and they take up a lot of space, along with the conveyor dryers and exposure units."

She could feel his head turn toward her, and his warm breath grazed her cheek.

He stood up straight and Diana did the same, taking a little step toward him. They were face-to-face, close enough for her to see the pupils of his eyes dilating. He had long eyelashes, slightly blonder than his brown hair. As he began to talk more about the building, it became a mumble to Diana, as she looked straight into his pretty blue eyes. They were the only thing about his body that was soft.

Diana wanted him and he could feel it too, because he stopped talking, looked at her, and smiled. She reached for his hand, and she placed it on her waist as she slid her own hand up his arm to his shoulder. Instantly he pulled her forward, not quite enough for a kiss, just enough for his eyes to be the only thing in her field of vision. There was the rush again, that moment just before the first kiss of someone new, and it excited her, it made her feel warm inside. A release of endorphins caused by the titillating excitement of anticipation made her feel high.

As he pulled her closer, she leaned her head back and could feel her breasts press up against his strong chest. There was an immediate sensation, as if their clothing were disintegrating and they were skin to skin in that instant. He leaned into her, pulled her head closer, and began kissing her with his firm lips. At first it was a polite soft kiss, and then he kissed her a little harder and a little longer. Their pulsing lips met slowly and deliberately until he tilted his head and kissed along the line of her jaw, down to the soft skin just below her ear. He pushed his nose against her and took a deep breath as he kissed down her neck.

Her face pressed against his shoulder, she could smell his cologne, more musky than before, and it made her nose tingle. His strong hands caressed her back until he moved them down and squeezed her rear. Ever so gently he lifted her up and crushed her toward him. Their bodies were closer now and he moved his hands up and along the curve of her back until he held her head, gently caressing her face.

Looking into her eyes for a sign of approval, he gave her a deep kiss and she could feel his warm tongue glide along her lips. Diana kissed him back and slipped her tongue between his lips until his breathing became heavy. She dropped her pea coat to the floor along with her sweater, kicked her shoes off and slipped off her jeans and underclothes. His hands fumbled to remove his navy blazer and topcoat all at once and then remove his pants. Down on the floor their clothes lay in a tangled embrace.

There were no words exchanged as Diana began to unbutton his crisp dress shirt. His chest was broad and smooth, and she could feel the warmth of his body as he laid her back on the desk. The whole time she watched him looking at her body, and it excited her to know that he wanted her. Carter ran his warm hands along her thighs to her waist and kissed the inside of her thigh near her knee. Ever so slowly he marched his tongue like a soldier to his conquest. He kissed her deeply there, until he could tell she wanted him. Their eyes met and, without looking down, he slipped into her.

Grabbing her around the waist, he pressed his body into hers, rocking into her and increasing his pace. Beneath her she could feel the stack of blueprints moving with his rhythm. The thought of him on her in this building and on this desk excited her to the edge of climax. Her breathing became heavier and she felt the crush of his body against her as he pushed harder until she felt his warmth release inside her. With a sudden intensity driven by the pulse of him within the wetness of her, her body exploded in a gorgeous rapture.

Carter had proven himself a more-than-adequate real estate agent, and this last property met all her requirements. It was a good price too. After they said good-bye in the parking lot and she watched him drive way, she was confident her offer would be accepted. He had all but guaranteed he could make it happen for her.

With a feeling of sublime success, she lit up another cigarette and called her husband Jack to tell him she had put a contract on the property. As she had so many times before, Diana the huntress had gotten what she wanted.

When she finished her cigarette, she drove her rental car back toward town. Along the way, among the warehouses that lined Washington Street, Diana passed by the old building that had once housed Strider's. In its glory days, it had been Charleston's premier venue for rock bands, hosting such acts as the Ramones, R.E.M., the Red Hot Chili Peppers, and local success story Hootie & the Blowfish. It was also here that Diana's band Crazy Hearts had played its farewell show before the band relocated to Nashville.

She had come a long way since those days and the nostalgia of it all caused her to pull over in front of the building, which had recently been chopped up into office spaces. While the facade had been dressed up, the industrial-looking double doors were still there, but permanently opened wide to reveal a breezeway with rows of doors to offices and commercial spaces. It was the antithesis of what it had been when the warehouse district was a collection of derelict buildings surrounded by a decaying neighborhood. Because of cheap rent and neighbors who were too poor to care, the large space had spent the eighties and nineties as a music hall where alternative rock 'n' roll bands played to young patrons marinated in cheap beer and stoned on drugs.

Crazy Hearts developed a faithful regional following and sold out the small venues around town and along the South Carolina coastline. It was Diana's last year in college and they played weekends, and though the money was not very good, she and her three bandmates rented an old warehouse to live and practice in and abandoned their part-time jobs. They also abandoned the idea of finding "real" jobs after college, and barely made it to graduation. Diana sang and played guitar, and the all-girl band played rocked-out versions of country and western songs. The Girls showed real promise, so much that a major recording label based out of Nashville picked up her and the girls.

The summer after graduation, the label prompted them to play a grueling series of nightly shows along the East Coast. The label wanted the unknown band to test its new material before it would be allowed to record its first album. It was a low-budget tour, with the band, one roadie, and their road manager, Diana's soon-to-be-husband Jack. The response was strong, and they sold thousands of T-shirts and gave the label what it wanted, an audience eager to buy the upcoming album.

The girls had given up their warehouse apartment for the tour and had sold or given away whatever they could not fit on the bus. They decided the band should give it its best shot and relocate to Nashville.

It was the last show they would ever play in Charleston and it was sold out. Jack had managed to get coverage for the band in the local papers, touting the success of its first major tour and promoting its new material. Hootie & the Blowfish had just hit the national charts and interest in Diana's band was intense. Everybody from the news media to live-music junkies wanted South Carolina to be the next Seattle.

It was the band's first headline show. It was no longer an opening act. A band called the Tantrums opened, and by the time the girls took the stage, the audience was pumped up and ready to go. To date it was the girls' biggest show and they felt like superstars as the audience chanted and stomped its feet for them to take the stage. The importance of this show was huge even before Jack identified a writer for *Rolling Stone* magazine in the crowd and pointed him out to the band. They were not a small-town band any longer. The arts and entertainment reporter with the Charleston *Post and Courier* and his photographer were hanging out to the right of the stage, talking with some young fans who were wearing the band's T-shirts. Backstage, Jack had even let a college kid with a video camera document the show and promised him interviews later in the night.

The girls came onstage after the lights dimmed and took their places. Behind the drummer Jack had set up a projection screen, and as soon as Diana gave the cue, the band's logo popped up in the darkness and Diana launched into a raucous version of Hank Williams's "Lost Highway." Diana sang, "Just another girl on the lost highway," and the big screen began rolling footage of the band on the road during its East Coast tour. Pictures of the band on the tour bus and at truck stops, cheap restaurants, and hotels narrated the low-budget tour. There were concert shots, and pictures of the band performing with the occasional country music guest star. The audience loved it and connected with the honest rock-infused country music.

Diana was wearing a very short denim skirt, with black cowboy boots and a flannel shirt unbuttoned to reveal her cleavage. Skyler, her bass player, wore jeans and a cowboy shirt, topped off with a white cowboy hat cocked on her head. Her electric guitar player Julie wore a blue Western-inspired dress and baby blue cowboy boots, while her drummer Annie wore a halter top, and a denim skirt as short as Diana's. The drummer's skirt rode up her legs as she sat on her stool, and revealed a heart tattoo on her left thigh. They all oozed tough-girl sex appeal.

The music was a raw and grungy rock approach to old-time country songs. Sometimes Julie played slide guitar to mimic the country twang, but mostly she played cowboy chords with distorted guitar, against Diana's clean acoustic rhythm guitar. Some of the revised country standards were unrecognizable. The band's sound was decidedly more hard rock than country, and reflective of the music coming out of the Seattle scene.

August can be very hot in Charleston, and this was one of those sweltering evenings. It had cooled to a tepid eighty-nine degrees, and the ocean-driven humidity filled the air like a dense salty soup. However, it did not seem to bother anyone. The band played through the fug of the dense air and the audience danced in a single mass of bodies soaked in sweat and beer.

It was fitting that the last song of the first set of cover songs ended with a punked-up version of "Ring of Fire." Diana did her best Johnny Cash imitation and the crowd sang along with the chorus. Excitement and electricity filled the warm air, and Jack was watching the *Rolling Stone* reporter bob up and down with the crowd. Now it was time for the band to begin its original material on an audience it held in the palms of its hands.

Diana finished the song and stepped back to grab her beer while the crowd applauded wildly.

"Thank you, Charleston!" Diana said. "That was Mr. Johnny Cash, country music's first punk rocker."

She was interrupted by a loud cheer and clapping, and she took the opportunity to chug her beer.

"Now, a whole lot of times, a band will take a break about now. But that's not us, because we want to keep the music coming."

The audience cheered again and Diana and her bandmates smiled at each other until the thunderous noise subsided.

"I know some of y'all may have heard we have a

record coming out soon, and tonight we'd like to play a few of our original songs from our upcoming album."

The drummer counted down, and the band launched into "First Blush," the first of its original songs.

She can't forget about that boy
She used to dance and sing for joy
Was long ago she fell in love
They fit like a hand in a glove
She was so young, but so was he
Had a love that was meant to be
She looks back as the years go by
Watching the tears fall from the sky

And at the first blush, it was her first crush
But the last time she fell in love
Her very first love, sent from God above
The only boy she really knew
It was long ago, and she's married to
Another man she never knew
She still regrets, and can't forget
It's not enough to have loved and lost

She knows she's got a good husband
But can't forget what might have been
Now she's grown with a little child
But remembers how big she smiled
It was a road she should have taken
Instead her life's rattled and shaken
How could she know what path to travel?
Now she watches her life unravel

And at the first blush, it was her first crush
But the last time she fell in love
Her very first love, sent from God above
The only boy she really knew
It was long ago, and she's married to
Another man she never knew
She still regrets, and can't forget
It's not enough to have loved and lost

The crowd was moving and gyrating with the music, and some of them were singing along during the last chorus even though they had just learned the words. They had connected with the music and the new material seemed to move them more than the rocked-out country standards the band was known for. The band played song after song, and the reaction was better than Jack had anticipated. It was the proof that everyone had been looking for, that this band was ready to record.

When the band finished its new songs, it punched out three encores, ending with a grungy version of Roy Orbison's "Only the Lonely (Know the Way I Feel)." When Diana and the girls finally left the stage, the audience was still chanting for more and stomping its feet, but the night had to end. The band had played for well over three hours without a break, and the girls were exhausted.

The rest of the night was a blur for all of them. They partied with the reporter from *Rolling Stone* magazine, took pictures with people who had slipped backstage, and drank themselves into a stupor. Backstage, a fog of pot smoke filled the air and hung like a great indoor cumulus cloud. The scene was very rock 'n' roll, and served as their introduction to the debauchery of rock star life.

Diana went up to everyone in the room, toasting with and consuming whatever they were drinking, and making sure they knew who she was. She wanted everyone to remember this night, and like a proud parent she would grab the closest member of the band and introduce her to whoever was in front of them. Against a brick wall painted black, Annie and Skyler were hanging on to each other, dancing, drinking, and kissing any boy who came up to them. As the night wore on Julie became manic, talking less and laughing more. It was their moment, the climax of the tour and a special farewell concert. They were crowned with the laurels they had earned from life on the road and working the nightclubs. They were ready for a shot at a bigger stage and they knew their record deal was sealed. It was time to kick back and celebrate.

The only one lucid the next morning was Jack. He had to be. As their manager, he had to pick up the check for the night's performance, load equipment into the tour bus, and verify hotel reservations and meeting times with the record label. The band was heading to Nashville to become the next big thing.

~2~

CHARLESTON EVE

Diana watched Jack pull up to the curb at the French Quarter Inn. The hotel was one of Charleston's finest and she had been staying there for the past couple of weeks. Surrounded by ancient buildings and over three hundred years of history, the hotel was elegant and comfortable. In what had once been the French Quarter of the old city, the adjoining blocks were a mix of colonial American edifices with European influences.

While her wardrobe and appearance were always uncomplicated and decidedly not reflective of her wealth, her choice of hotels was quite the opposite. She adored beautiful hotels and searched out the best that any city she visited had to offer. While she was happy with Levi's, never spending more than fifty dollars on a pair of jeans, she would easily plop down a thousand dollars or more for a hotel room. She pampered herself in the way she lived, not the way she dressed.

Diana flagged down a valet and sent him over to her husband. The valet was an older man with permanent sunburn who had made a career out of parking cars and checking luggage. It was therefore with much pomp that he opened the door of Jack's silver Toyota Spyder and welcomed him to the hotel. As he wrote out a parking card, Jack reached over and retrieved his duffel bag and briefcase from the front seat. The attendant offered to take it, but Jack politely refused and slipped the old man a few dollars before walking over to Diana.

"Hey, baby, how was the drive?"

"Long." Jack set his bag and briefcase down on the sidewalk. He was expressive and always talked with his hands.

"But it wasn't as long as the two weeks me and the kids were without you."

He cracked a little smile and she smiled back at him.

Jack had many wonderful qualities, and his best attribute was his sweetness. There was softness about him. He had dark wavy hair that was thick, and though he shaved every day, he always had a little soft stubble on his face. This and the comfortable way he dressed caused him to look as if he'd be at home in a log cabin. He was wearing his old Adirondack barn coat, a plaid shirt, and his old tweed cap.

The two had a similar style with clothing. It was one of the few things that gave them away as a married couple. They lived similarly, but loved differently.

Jack was a good man, and Diana knew that. He was a caring father, and an affectionate and faithful husband. Fidelity may have been a flexible idea with her, often nonexistent, but she knew with 100 percent certainty that he was true to her, and was still madly in love with her after twenty years. While there were moments when these thoughts panged her heart, those moments were short and buffered by her lust for life.

"How about we drop off your bags and then go get some dinner?"

"Sounds like a plan," he said.

Jack picked up his duffel bag, slung it over his shoulder, and snatched up his briefcase.

"There's a restaurant in the hotel, but Magnolias is still open. Do you remember that place?"

"Yeah, I remember it. Let's go there."

Diana and Jack stepped into the hotel, only to emerge through the front door ten minutes later. He took her hand as they hit the street, merging with the tourists and residents on their way to dinner. The coming dusk gave dimension to their easy walk, and the long shadows from the setting sun cast shafts of light between the buildings.

"Meant to ask, did you remember to bring my little red box with the Chinese dragon on it?"

A random shaft of setting sunlight lit up her hair and face.

"Yes, I did, it's in my bag."

"Thank you, babe," she said, and put her arm around him. "The weather finally warmed up a bit. It was so cold last week."

"It was cold back home too. Now I have my love to keep me warm."

Jack kissed her on the cheek. He had always enjoyed incorporating song lyrics into their conversations and was especially fond of quoting Irving Berlin and Cole Porter.

"I'm excited to see the new place. David and I

have already done a layout of how to arrange the equipment."

"We have an appointment tomorrow at ten with Carter. He's the agent."

They walked down Linguard Street to State Street and stopped by a traffic light, waiting to cross. Jack surveyed the area and felt at home, which caused a big grin to rise across his face.

"He'll be there to unlock the door," she said, "and let the building inspector and electrician in for their inspections. Then that afternoon, at three o'clock, we meet with the attorney to go over the contract, restrictive covenants, city regulations, and any other concerns."

Traffic came to a stop and the two stepped through an opening between cars and crossed the street.

"As long as the inspectors don't find any problems, and we are okay with the lawyer stuff, we should be ready to close next week."

Jack, who was always a good listener, was nodding his head. He grasped her hand and led her through a small crowd of people headed their way.

"The sooner we can get started the better," he said. "I don't want to order the equipment until after we close."

A block and a half farther along State Street, they turned left on Lodge Street and marched down toward East Bay. As the sun's light began to fade, the lights of the Holy City began to flicker on one by one. East Bay Street was bumper-to-bumper with cars and the headlights were flickering like low-lying stars. The city was alive with people on their way to dinner.

Walking a couple of blocks more, they saw a

young couple coming down the steps of Magnolias, smiling with dreamy eyes toward one another. Jack stopped Diana in front of one of the big windows made amber with the very last bit of the setting sun.

"I can't believe this place is still here," he said. "I remember when it first opened. It used to be our restaurant. Not that we ate here much, since we never had any money."

Jack gave her a hug and looked around at the old familiar buildings. Some of the names of the shops and cafés had changed, but the streetscape was still very much the same. As a car passed by, its headlights lit up his face for a brief instant. Diana had always loved the little lines on the sides of his mouth when he smiled, and now the lines were more prominent.

"It's nice to be back," he said. "This place is comfortable. Like being home."

"Here at Magnolias?" she asked.

"No. Here in Charleston."

Diana put her hands on her hips, cocked her head to one side, and cracked a smile.

"Sweetheart," he said, "you know there's nothing keeping us in Nashville. Well, maybe your mom. David can totally manage the shop. He virtually ran the place when we were in China last year." Jack was in sell mode, making a case for something brewing in his mind. "Then there's the fact that one of us would have to stay here for at least six months to start this new operation."

He offered her a warm inviting smile.

"What if we moved here? Permanently."

She smiled at him and gave him a quick burst of laughter, almost as if she had just heard a joke. "Really? What about the kids?"

"I think they would love to be here, warmer weather, historic city, and of course the beaches."

"That could be good for them," she said. "Maybe they'd spend more time outside than on the computer and video games. I also agree that David can run the Nashville operations."

"Let's give it some thought." He grabbed her hands, pulled her close to him, and looked into her eyes. "Tomorrow you can ask that hotshot real estate agent of yours about the housing market here in town."

She gave him a little smile and kissed him. "Well, okay. We can look around, see what's available."

She was excited in the way that makes one's thoughts wander toward what-ifs and other possibilities. A change of scenery would be good for them and would take her away from the drama of her mother's pending divorce from her fourth husband.

He took her hand and the two walked up the steps and went inside Magnolias. The restaurant was humming with activity, and the din of mixed conversations was all one sound. After a short wait, they approached the hostess, who nervously tapped her pen on top of the stand. Jack held up two fingers and told her their name. She scanned the grease-pencil-smudged seating chart and told them the wait was about fifteen minutes, and wrote down, "Parks, party of two." She asked them to have a seat at the bar, which of course had no seats available because the waiting area was a small crowd of people waiting for tables.

The place was busy for a Wednesday night. Every table was filled and there was even a private party in the wine room. From the elevated area of the bar they could see the maze-like layout of tables and watch the waitstaff navigate like little mice in search of cheese.

When the hostess called the couple standing near them and led them to their table, Diana and Jack shifted into their vacant space. She heard the door open and felt a cold gust of wind slip into the restaurant. She looked over her shoulder in a passing glance, and returned to facing forward. Then there was a moment of recognition, and she turned her head back around, letting out a shriek.

"Oh my God. Eve?"

Instantly recognizing Diana, Eve Hayes dropped her single-woman-out-alone facade and bounded over to where Diana and Jack were standing. Her motions were graceful because of her tall and lean athletic figure.

Eve's eyes sometimes looked blue-green and other times shone with a green iridescent shimmer against the paleness of her skin. Her naturally light-blond hair, cut in a modern take on a pageboy, gave her an edgy and artsy look. However, Eve was neither edgy nor artsy, and her grace of movement was a happy accident from Mother Nature. She was wearing her office clothes: a smart gray flannel skirt that hung just below her knees, a lavender cotton blouse buttoned all the way up, a double-breasted wool jacket with a high collar, and a belt that matched her skirt. In her hands she held a small Burberry handbag.

"Diana. It can't be…what the heck are you doing in town?"

"I'm here on business with my husband." Diana thought for a moment. "You know, I don't think you ever met him when we were in college." Diana grabbed Jack by the shoulder. "Eve, this is my husband Jack, and honey, this is Eve, one of my friends from college."

"It's very nice to meet you," Eve said.

"Me too, it's a pleasure," Jack said.

"Eve, you remember Folly Beach. Those were some great times."

"They were, weren't they?" Eve said. "Wait. Is this the Jack that was your number one groupie? The T-shirt guy?"

Jack leaned over to Eve and gave her a big hug, taking her aback, since she was not the hugging type. "Yep, that's me." He nodded his head in mock embarrassment. "I'm the T-shirt guy."

Diana was looking around. "Eve, are you here with someone?"

"No, just me." Eve held up her hand as if to single herself out. "Table for one."

Eve laughed at her joke. It was a nervous habit she had recently developed. Whenever she tried to be witty, she would always laugh at herself, just to make sure that others knew she was being funny.

"Didn't you marry Professor Hayes?" Diana asked. "Where is he tonight?"

"Porter. Porter Hayes, and yes, we were married, but he died last year."

Diana, who always looked as if she was just about to laugh at someone's joke, grew quickly somber. "Oh, sweetheart, I'm so sorry."

"Don't be, it's okay. He died in his sleep. A sudden heart attack. There was no misery in his passing." Eve stuttered for a moment, realizing what she had said. "Oh God. That sounded so morose. I mean to say there was no misery for him. The doctor told me he didn't feel anything."

Eve looked a little self-conscious. Jack caught on and seized the opportunity. "Hey, the T-shirt guy would like for you to dine with us," he said with a childlike smirk.

"Thank you, but no. I don't want to be a third wheel."

Always the nice guy, Jack walked over to the hostess stand to change the number of their party to three. He returned as quickly as he'd left. "See, no problem."

Minutes after Jack altered the reservations, a slim-hipped girl carrying three oversize menus called out, "Parks! Party of three."

Diana, trailed by Eve and then Jack, followed the waif of a college girl through the crowded restaurant. The young girl was dressed in black pencil pants and a black turtleneck sweater. Her thin limbs and mechanical movements made her look like some kind of windup doll moving through the crowded restaurant, oblivious to everyone. Diana imagined that she was either wretchedly vacant or coolly aloof, and for the girl's sake, she hoped it was the latter.

The hostess led them to a four-top table beneath a large painting of a magnolia blossom. Jack pulled out a chair for Diana and she sat down against the wall. He removed his jacket, placed it on the back of his chair, and sat beside her. Eve sat across from Diana.

After the hostess doled out the menus she said, "Your waitress will be here soon," and promptly left the table just as mechanically as she had led them to it.

"I am very sorry to hear about your husband passing away," Diana said. She turned to Jack. "He was an English professor here at the college. Eve and

I had him for comparative literature."

"Those were the days," Eve said.

"Didn't you move in with him after spring break? He had that cute little house across the street from the humanities building."

"I sold that place after he passed away," Eve said. "Everything was hard at first. I actually just bought a new house."

Eve picked up her wineglass and looked for spots.

"Did the memories of your old place make it too difficult to live there?" Jack asked.

"No. Well, yes, but the main reason was for my son."

"You have a son?" Diana said.

"We had one child right after we were married. I carried him while starting graduate school at USC. Porter got a position there and it worked out for me because I was able to earn my PhD in psych." Eve took her silverware and unconsciously began wiping the fork, then the knife and spoon, with her napkin. "Malcolm. His name is Malcolm and he's so creative. He just turned twenty and after a year at SCAD he's decided he doesn't need art school to be an artist. My new house has an apartment in the back and he's living there."

"SCAD? That's my alma mater," Jack said. "What kind of medium does he use?"

"He's a visual artist, and he's also been composing music. Sometimes he reminds me so much of Porter."

"I remember Professor Hayes so clearly." Diana placed her napkin on her lap. "He always wore a bow tie, a real good-looking guy too." Diana turned to Jack and said, "He had a thing for the plays of Oscar Wilde and would quote him all the time."

"A thing? You think?" Eve perked up. "More like an obsession," she said with a laugh. "The work that made his career was an annotated collection of all of Wilde's plays. It's the reason the College of Charleston wooed him back as dean of humanities."

"Interesting," Jack said. "The only thing I ever read by Oscar Wilde was *The Picture of Dorian Gray*. It was an admitted attempt at irony by one of my fine arts professors. He was also a devotee of the English school of painters and Walter Pater. Arts for art's sake."

"Like I haven't heard that a million times. And, this is too funny," Eve added, "Malcolm would always walk around at breakfast yelling, 'A Pop-Tart for art's sake.'"

"Eve, what about you? What do you do?" Jack asked.

"I teach psychology at the College of Charleston. Occasionally I'm involved in clinical research when I can get grant money, but with the economy the way it is, it's been tough." Eve smiled with a sparkle in her eye. "But my latest thing, and I'm very excited about this, is a talk show on educational radio. We just went statewide three months ago. The show's on Monday and Thursday afternoons from one till three thirty."

"What's your show about?" asked Diana.

"Relationships," Eve said. "Love, marriage, dating, I cover it all. I feel like I'm actually helping people. You know. There's too much emphasis placed on all of these romantic ideals perpetuated by Hallmark and Hollywood. The divorce rate would be cut in half if people realized that a relationship is as much of an agreement and contract as it is about feelings of love and romance."

Not wanting to get into a debate about love and romance, Diana suggested that they place their order, and flagged the long-overdue waitress to their table. She was an apple-cheeked blonde who was as excited to be working tonight as the hostess was. Her necktie was tucked into her white Oxford shirt. She rattled off a list of specials, none of which was special enough to order.

Diana ordered the blackened salmon with saffron risotto, and Jack ordered the blue crab–stuffed rainbow trout with collard greens, both of which came with salad. After some indecision, Eve ordered a cup of tomato bisque as her entrée. Diana ordered a bottle of Louis Jadot Chardonnay for the table.

Once the waitress left, Eve looked at her friend inquisitively.

"Diana, are you still performing? Your band was called Crazy Hearts, right?"

"Yeah, that's right, Crazy Hearts. And no, my touring days are over. The band broke up about a year and a half after moving to Nashville."

"Aw, that's a shame. Your band turned country and bluegrass into rock songs. 'Country grunge' they called it. Right? And you had a record too?"

"Yes. Actually recorded two records and three songs from the first album charted, one even reached the country top ten. We disbanded at the end of the second tour."

"So, tell me. What happened?" Eve leaned over the table. "Tell me the scoop. Someone in the band have addiction issues? Heavy drinking? Bad blood? Was it one of those rock band things?"

"It was me, the T-shirt guy," Jack said. "I broke up the band. I am Yoko."

Diana lovingly slapped Jack on the shoulder and he laughed.

"Oh Jack, stop. It's not what you think. I don't know if I ever told you the real story of how Jack and I met."

"No. Other than he was the guy who showed up at all of your shows selling T-shirts. That he was chasing you around. That he was the 'Every Breath You Take' guy."

"Well, that's part of it. Jack had seen our band when he was at SCAD."

"That's when I fell in love with her," Jack said.

Diana hushed him. "Let me tell the story," she said. "So he leaves school and moves in with his brother here in Charleston. He told me it was because he wanted to be near me, which was so sweet. Without a job, the only way for him to support himself was by selling T-shirts he designed and printed. One night after one of our shows, Jack approached us about making T-shirts for the band. We agreed and he also became our first roadie."

The waitress, who carried the wine and salads, interrupted Diana.

"When we signed a deal with Capitol Records he became our manager, and we went to Nashville to cut our first record. We got married after we cut our last track and played the Nashville clubs, before the label sent us on a national tour. At the same time, Jack handled our merchandising and set up a screen printing place in Nashville. Funny thing was, while we made decent money from record sales, we made more money by selling our own T-shirts and other merchandise."

Jack finished his salad and interrupted her. "You

have to understand that a lot of bands break even or even lose money on a tour. It's really a way to support album sales, and bands usually pay for their own music videos and other such things." Jack took a sip of his wine and continued, "So, let's say a band sells a respectable three hundred thousand copies over eighteen months. A young band may net a little over a dollar on each album, and split four ways, after expenses, agents, and legal, it's not a lot. We were selling our shirts for twenty bucks a pop and they were costing five each to make. The Internet was just heating up and we sold a lot that way too."

"Jack had designed a logo for our band," Diana said. It was a heart in a straitjacket. Even people who didn't know our music were buying them. A lot of young girls were wearing them as a fashion statement." Diana started to laugh. "Kind of disheartening when your band's logo is worth more than your music."

The waitress came to their table, refilled their wineglasses, and took their salad plates away.

"When the second tour ended and we started talking about a third album, we realized how big the T-shirt business had become, and I decided to call it quits with the band. With my mother's contacts we were able to get some big-name clients and the business grew and grew, and now we've got a large printing operation in Nashville and just put a contract on a second facility here in Charleston."

"That's why we are here," Jack said.

"And if Jack has his way we may even move here," Diana said.

"That's freaking amazing," Eve said. "All because of Jack's infatuation with you. See, love and business can go hand in hand."

"Ahhh, but the love came first," said Jack.

The apple-cheeked waitress arrived at their table carrying Jack and Diana's entrées. A young man with brown eyes and medium-length sandy-blond hair assisted her. He seemed out of place, more akin to a teen hanging out on the beach. He was carrying Eve's bisque and a long wooden pepper mill. He stood alongside the waitress, staring at Diana, as the waitress placed their food on the table. She motioned for him and he passed her the cup of bisque, which she placed in front of Eve.

As Diana and Jack were commenting on their food to one another, Eve was watching the young surfer dude stare at Diana. Eve had never thought of Diana as a woman men would ogle, not in college and not now. She was attractive, yes, but nothing about her stood out. This made Eve's observation of this young man even more interesting.

Before the waitstaff duo left the table, the young man presented his pepper mill with two hands, as if climbing a rope. He asked if anyone would like fresh pepper and both Eve and Diana said yes. He ground a little into Eve's bisque with a little quick turn of the wrist. Pointing the long peppermill toward Diana, he took pleasure in adding pepper for her with long slow twists. Eve smiled, almost chuckled to herself, and began eating her tomato bisque.

Eve had always dined in measured steps, eating small portions in a somewhat mechanical fashion. She also exercised and loved to swim all year round at the college pool complex. Her thin and athletic body was testament to her daily routine and diet. On the other hand, Diana ate with gusto, and like Jack she enjoyed rich foods and generous portions. She consumed her meals with a passion for finer things, and savored her food as she savored life. Very often Diana and Jack would feed each other, sharing their food and opinions.

"Oh my God, Diana, try this," he said. "The blue crab stuffing is so good."

Jack scooped up a portion of the crab-and-cornbread mix on his fork and fed it to Diana. Her mouth was wide open like a baby bird's. She closed her eyes as she chewed and tasted this savory bit.

"Oh yeah. That is soooo good," Diana said. "Here, you have to try my saffron risotto."

Diana fed Jack a yellow fluffy portion of risotto, and all he could say was, "Mmmmm."

"I can't wait to tell Lucy I ran into you," Eve said as she finished her meager soup.

"Lucy?" Diana said. "I'd almost forgotten to ask. I'm guessing she's still here, since her family practically founded Charleston." Diana turned to Jack. "Lucy was my other college friend I've told you about, the one whose family had the house on Folly Beach, but she grew up in one of those huge ancient houses on the Battery."

"She's living there now."

"At Folly?" Diana asked.

"Oh no, she and her husband and sons are living in the old house on the Battery. When her husband left the marine corps and they moved back to town, her mother gave them the house. She had lived there all alone after Lucy's father died."

"That's the last time I spoke to her. I had heard the news but was out of town and couldn't be there for the funeral. Is her mother still alive?"

"No, her mother died about five years ago. She was living at the beach house then."

"Ah, that's a shame. You say Lucy has sons?"

"Yes, twin boys, both first-year cadets at the Citadel. Her husband went there too. You might remember him. He was one of the Citadel boys next door during that first summer at Folly."

"My mind is very foggy about that summer." Diana mildly laughed. "Do you see her much?"

"About once a week for lunch."

"And what is she doing now?" Diana asked.

"You know, a lot of the same things her mother did." Eve sipped her last bit of wine. "Garden Club, Junior League, volunteering at the church. Her husband travels a lot with his job, and now that her sons are in college, she's got a very active social life."

Diana was nodding her head. "What about Maggie? Anything from her?"

"I haven't seen her since she left town," Eve said, "but do you remember Professor Hyatt in philosophy? She kept in touch with her for a little while and said when she left school she went to teach English somewhere in China."

"Maggie was the one who got me interested in playing guitar," Diana said to Jack.

"I remember you talking about her," he said. He thought for a moment, trying to recall a detail. "She's the one who wanted everything pink. Right?"

"Yeah, that's right, pink clothes, pink car, pink everything."

Jack was finishing his meal when the waitress came by to clear the table. The young girl picked up their empty plates and asked if they wanted dessert. Eve said no and Diana and Jack both said yes. When the waitress returned, Eve never bothered to look at the dessert menu, but Diana studied it and listened with interest to the dessert specials.

"I'll have decaffeinated coffee," Eve said, "and could you please bring me skim milk? Not two percent but skim, please. Okay?"

The waitress nodded and asked Diana what she would like.

"Jack, do you want to split a piece of chocolate cake?"

Jack smiled at her. "Yes, that'd be great. Three forks, please."

The waitress collected their menus and scurried away.

"I hope the third fork is not for me," Eve said. "I don't do sugar."

"Don't do sugar? Are you kidding?" Jack seemed amused.

"Her mother was a dentist," Diana told Jack.

"Besides rotting your teeth out, it's just bad for your body. Sugar is poison. It's never been a thing for me."

"Well, okay then," Jack said, almost smirking.

Shortly thereafter the young waiter who had wielded the pepper mill arrived at their table with a tall slice of chocolate cake. He gingerly placed it in front of Diana and smiled. He turned to Eve and placed her coffee and milk in front of her with a single simple gesture. He mumbled something snarky about coffee for dessert, but he told Diana he hoped she enjoyed her cake.

"What's wrong with that kid?" Eve was smirking and thinking aloud.

"Teenager stuff," Jack said. "We have two

ourselves that I can't ever figure out."

Eve poured her skim milk and stirred her coffee. "Two? Really? How old are they?"

"A boy and a girl," Jack said. "Our son Seth is—"

He stopped short as Diana fed him a bite of chocolate cake.

"Seth is sixteen and is just learning to drive," Diana said. "Samantha is seventeen and has the whole boy-crazy approach to every—"

Jack interrupted Diana by stuffing an even bigger bite of chocolate cake into her mouth. He laughed as she tried to continue talking with her mouth full, incomprehensibly to Eve.

Eve playfully rolled her eyes, in part because of their silly romantic gestures, but mostly to cover her antipathy to the two feeding one another. "Look at you two, having such a romantic exchange of germs," she said. She was partly joking, but her tone was serious.

Jack just smiled back at her as he fed Diana more cake. "As a psychologist I would think you would see it as someone nourishing their love for someone."

"Perhaps," Eve said, "or neediness, or, as I said, a romantic gesture of germs."

"I love it when my man feeds me," Diana said, "especially chocolate."

Diana and Jack ate their cake and Eve sipped her skim milk–laden decaffeinated coffee. They exchanged small talk and after a handful of tourists passed by on their way to a newly bussed table, the apple-cheeked waitress came over with their check. She placed it in the middle of the table and Jack immediately reached for it. "Allow me," he said.

"No, I want to pay my part," Eve said. She tried to

see the receipt, but Jack prevented her.

"I insist. We invited you to eat with us. Besides, your part would be like me adding a cup of soup to my dinner and coffee afterward. You're a cheap date."

"Let him take care of it," Diana said. "I always have him pay for everything." She chuckled.

"Well, okay," Eve said, "but next time it will be my treat."

Jack pulled out his wallet, flipped through various cards, and slipped out his credit card, placing it in the slot of the cardholder along with the bill.

"Diana?" Eve said. "How much longer are you going to be in town?"

"Until the end of next week. We're on a fast track to close on the new property, and I believe Jack wants to check out a few houses this weekend." She turned to Jack. "Is that right, honey?"

"We can see what our money will buy us here in Charleston," he said. He was smiling, like a kid about to get candy.

"What's your schedule like?" Eve asked.

"Tied up between now and the weekend, and if all goes as planned, we should close on Tuesday of next week." Diana thought for a moment. "So far nothing planned for Monday. Why do you ask?"

"I'm supposed to meet Lucy for lunch on Saturday," Eve said. "And I was thinking of seeing if she can reschedule. Maybe the three of us could meet Monday afternoon, say four o'clock, after my radio show?"

"Oh yeah? That'd be great, I'd like that, but I wouldn't want to intrude."

"I know she'd love to see you. We meet at each other's house, and it's her turn. She usually makes quiche."

Before they could complete their plans, the waitress brought the bill and Jack's credit card back to the table. At the end of this momentary pause, Eve pulled a phone out of her Burberry bag and deftly placed her fingers over the screen, like a runner waiting for the start of a race. "What's your mobile number?" she asked.

Diana recited her number to Eve and asked her for hers, scribbling it on one of the square cocktail napkins.

"I'll speak to Lucy tomorrow and give you a call to confirm."

Jack stood up and slipped on his coat. He took Diana's hand and helped her up as Eve stood up clutching her bag. The three made their way past a few tables, and up the ramp toward the front door. The restaurant crowd had thinned out and the once-busy restaurant staff was now idle. When they passed the hostess stand, the slim-hipped hostess was gossiping with the apple-cheeked waitress.

When Diana, Jack, and Eve exited the building, a sudden gust of wind made Eve cower with cold and she pulled up her collar. The air was crisp, like a bite out of an ice-cold Granny Smith apple. Night had fallen and the amber lights gave the streetscape a deceptively warm glow.

"Diana, I'm so glad I ran into you, I know Lucy will feel the same. It would be wonderful if you moved here."

"It was great seeing you too, brought back a flood of memories."

Diana smiled at her and Jack chimed in, "And we are going to give moving here some serious thought."

Diana reached over and gave Eve a hug good-bye, but Eve was not the kind of woman who was fond of hugs. Jack did the same, completely taking Eve out of her comfort zone.

"Bye, honey," Diana said. She grabbed Jack's arm and pulled him close to her. Eve gave a polite wave and smiled before walking back to her car.

WALTZING in VIENNA

~3~

TEA WITH LUCY

“ “This afternoon, join Olivia Ashley on *The State of Opera* with a rebroadcast of Mozart’s *Don Giovanni* performed at Dock Street Theatre during last year’s Spoleto Festival. Today at four o’clock on ETV Radio, WSCI Charleston, eighty-nine point three.” As the promo ended, the production assistant meticulously watched the countdown and checked audio levels on the computer monitors that surrounded her. She was a studious-looking girl, barely out of college, and her thin eyeglasses seemed as if they were attached to her headphones, the whole looking like big mechanical headgear. Her hair was in a carefree bob, and her clothing and look were those of a librarian, or a production assistant for educational radio, which she was. Her hands were poised on the slider switches of a large audio console that lay in front of her.

Eve Hayes was sitting at the radio desk opposite the production assistant. She was wearing a cream-colored pantsuit trimmed in piping that was slightly creamier than the fabric. Her head was crowned by a pair of studio headphones. In front of her were her notes for the show, production papers stacked neatly on the desk, and a microphone on a boom that floated in front of her face. To her right sat a bottle of water and a small container of plain Greek yogurt.

As the production assistant switched over to the live feed, she quietly nodded her head and counted to herself—three, two, one—and then waved her hand at Eve as the cue to begin speaking.

"Welcome back for the second half of *The Psychology of Relationships*. I'm your host, Dr. Eve Hayes, professor of psychology at the College of Charleston."

Eve paused and the production assistant punched in the ten-second music cue for Eve's show.

"On the phone today," Eve said, "I'm joined by Dr. Howard Baskins, author of *Age and Relationships: The Benefits of Inequality*. Welcome back, Dr. Baskins."

"Thank you, Dr. Hayes," was the reply from the other end of the telephone connection.

"Dr. Baskins, on the first half of the show, we covered the basic principles of your book. I'd like to turn our attention to the response your theories have received from other academics and the public. For example, Dr. Ellen Goldstein has written that your book 'perpetuates sexual stereotypes' and 'could validate unhealthy relationships.' James Andrews with the *New York Times* said your book 'ignores human emotion' and 'disregards the notions of romance and love.' How do you respond to that?"

"Well," he said, "my proposition that younger women should marry older men is motivated by the fact that in most cases, older men make better providers. It's beneficial for both the young woman and their future children. I never suggested it was validation for dirty old men."

"Yes, of course," Eve said.

"Secondly," the voice said, "I find Mr. Andrews's comment a little biased since he can't fathom the idea that a twenty-one-year-old man can fall in love with a forty-year-old woman. Now, that's sexist if you ask me. Besides, a relationship like that forces the young man to be more responsible and mature, while providing the older woman with a husband who has greater virility and superior physical security and protection."

"Dr. Baskins," Eve said, "while I do see the benefits of many of the points you raise, not all relationships can be that pragmatic. Their criticism has merit, since relationships are formed by human bonds. However, as an overall concept, your work serves as a foundation for the practicality of certain relationships. Most of my listeners already know that my deceased husband was much older than I was. My particular relationship benefited me with a loving husband who provided the opportunity for me to attend graduate school and develop a career. Together we raised a healthy and happy son. Our relationship was one that began with love, and not because my deceased husband was lustfully looking for younger women."

"My book was never meant to be a literal guide, but rather a sensible view that age should not be a barrier in relationships. The age parameters I detail are based upon statistically verified data and, overall, make for a better society. Like in your case. Your relationship obviously gave you, as a young woman, a foundation of financial security and support to become a confident professional."

"Thank you, Dr. Baskins." Eve took a sip of water and continued. "At this time I'd like to take a few phone calls from our listeners. We already have a few folks in the queue." Eve flipped a switch on her control board. "Go ahead, caller number one."

"Yes, good afternoon," said the male caller. "I'd like to ask Dr. Baskins exactly how a relationship between a much older man with a younger woman is beneficial for, say, their, let's say their son?"

Eve's pale skin began to develop a reddish hue and she felt her mouth began to clench. She was awash with embarrassment and anger. It was a cringe, a full-body cringe.

She recognized the voice, and it was not the first time this person had called her show.

"Well, sir," Dr. Baskins said, "the obvious answer is that the environment the older father provides, in most cases, is more stable and financially secure. The older father is more established and presents a mature example for the child or children."

"Don't you think a relationship like that puts the burden on the woman," caller one said, "creating a separation of duties in child-rearing, and a loss of compassion by the father? It creates a maladaptive pattern of behavior in both parents. It's horribly misogynic, and…"

"Thank you, caller number one," Eve said. She punched her control button angrily, ending the call. "So as to give everyone a chance to call in, I want to move on to the next caller." Eve pressed the flashing button, her fingers nervously twitching. "Go ahead, caller number two."

"Hi, Dr. Hayes, this is Sarah, you know, from last

week? I just love your show. Oh, yeah, I have a question for Dr. Baskins about—"

The caller droned a question as Eve's thoughts drifted off. Dr. Baskins answered Sarah's question as he did for the next six callers, until the show's end. Eve was despondent because of the frustration and anger that swelled up inside her from caller number one. She ended her show mechanically, trying to contain her emotions.

After the show wrapped up, she left the studio and walked to her car. Out of earshot of anyone, Eve pulled out her phone and punched in a number.

"Malcolm! What in the heck was that about! I've told you before. Never call me during the show, especially pretending to be a listener." Eve ranted on as she walked through the parking lot. "That was embarrassing and could hurt my reputation as well as even cause me to lose this job."

Eve listened to his explanation on the other end of the phone, her cheeks red and her face tense with anger.

"Okay, I get it. You want to blame me for your failures?"

As she listened to the explanation her face loosened up, and her eyes began to water.

"Malcolm. I know. I know this has a lot to do with the loss of your father." Eve began to cry a little. "But sweetheart, I am here for you."

Eve listened to Malcolm as she walked up to her navy blue Volvo sedan. She sat in the driver's seat.

"I know, I know, don't get upset. Uh-huh, it's not your fault. It's going to be fine."

She paused to listen to her son a little more. She could not visualize him as a twenty-year-old man.

Instead his familiar voice reminded her of when he was five years old and entering kindergarten. Soon compassion for her son wiped away her tears and frustration.

"Yes, you can borrow my car. I'm headed to Lucy's house, so I should be home by seven or eight."

She paused sympathetically as he talked.

"Okay, I love you too. Bye-bye."

She flipped down the visor and used the attached mirror to wipe her eyes with a tissue. She applied a little pale lipstick and smiled at herself, not because she was happy, but because she wanted to make sure there was no lipstick on her teeth. Once she was satisfied with her appearance, she backed her car out of her parking space and maneuvered her sedan through the parked cars.

The drive to the Battery relaxed her and calmed her nerves. She felt composed again. Driving had always relaxed her. As a frustrated teen living with her parents, she would take long drives to clear her head. She had occasionally taken these drives while married to Porter, never voicing her complaints, but rather taking *her* drives for *her* time.

She knew all the scenic roads around town. They were like old friends who would console her. There was Ashley River Road, lined with magnificent mansions, magnolia trees, and live oaks draped with Spanish moss. It was a favorite in spring when the azaleas would bloom. Sometimes she took a short drive along Rainbow Row, other times she would head for Kiawah Island and drive under the arms of the majestic trees stretching over Bohicket Road. Very often her drives took her to the Battery, where she would follow the road along the great seawall separating Charleston Harbor and White Point Garden. She had always admired the grand antebellum homes that overlooked the park and the harbor. She had always imagined living in one of the Battery mansions.

Eve turned on to South Battery Street from Meeting Street and passed five stately homes holding court over the park. She turned into the familiar driveway of Lucy's house, past the gate of brick and wrought iron, and parked her car in back.

Lucy always kept her back door locked, so visitors, even family, had to enter from the front door. The three-story yellow masonry house was an Italianate masterpiece. The narrow columns and railings were trimmed in white, with double porches lining the front of the house.

Eve passed a large round fountain with a cherub holding a duck that poured water into a grey bowl stained with streaks of green algae. The fountain sat atop three intertwined concrete palmetto tree trunks, centered on the walkway that lead to the front porch. A few steps more and she faced the great mahogany front door.

Eve's slender finger pressed the doorbell and she could hear the muffled ring within the house. Within a minute Lucy appeared at the door. She had been born Lucille Marie Bonneau and she was a native Charlestonian. The idea of being a native may mean little to people who were not born in Charleston, but for the city's residents it is at the core of one's being. It marks a person as one of the truest of all Southerners, in both character and culture.

Lucy's ancestors had been French Huguenots who settled in the new English colony of Carolina in 1686, just after Charles Towne, as it was known then, was founded. Steadfast in their Protestant beliefs, her Huguenot ancestors had left France after the Revocation of the Edict of Nantes. Her family was proud of its religion, of being French, and most of all of being native Charlestonians. Lucy was proud to be a native, but she had broken one tradition. She had married a non-Huguenot. Her husband was Theodore Pendleton, an Episcopalian, but of course he was from another long line of native Charlestonians whose family dated back to ten years before the Huguenots' arrival. This fact had made their marriage easier to swallow for Lucy's family.

Jean-David Bonneau, who had amassed a fortune importing luxury European goods for wealthy planters, built the family house on South Battery Street in 1842. Monsieur Bonneau, known for his grand house and lavish parties, was also a noted photographer. After seeing an exhibition of the newly invented daguerreotype, he became a passionate practitioner of photography. During the Confederate War, Bonneau documented much of the action that took place in and around Charleston, and his work as well known as that of Union photographer Matthew Brady. His photographs serve as some of the best images of the war-torn South and the destruction of Charleston by the Yankees.

Though Lucy was a year younger than Eve and Diana, she looked much older. In particular this was because of the conservative way in which she dressed, and because she still wore pantyhose. Her idea of dressing down was to omit them while still dressing like a lady. Lucy had beautiful long dark hair, but it was in a dated hairstyle. Her very French brown eyes, despite her never taking the time to accentuate or enhance them, were her most striking feature. Indeed, her conservative skirt and silk blouse hid her voluptuous body. She was very much a Charleston lady and a Southern socialite.

"Oh darling, there you are," Lucy said. She still spoke in that slow Charleston style from the old South. "Come on in. Diana arrived earlier and she's been catching me up on her adventures in the band and T-shirt business. Interesting stuff. Don't you think?"

Eve nodded as she walked into the hallway. Entering the house was like entering a museum, with its wooden floors polished to perfection and its white plaster walls covered with dozens of photographs of Charleston from the late nineteenth century. They were the work of Monsieur Bonneau.

"We are in the family room," Lucy said.

They passed by the dining room, and then wisped past the brick-lined kitchen.

Eve heard one of Lucy's favorite piano concertos playing softly in the background as they entered the pale-gray walls of the family room. It was a selection from Bach's *Goldberg Variations*. Eve was also fond of Bach's piano compositions and they usually gave her a sense of calm, but today there was no calm..

Centered at the back of the room was a working coal-burning fireplace. Above it was a family portrait, a commissioned painting of Lucy and her husband Theo with their twin boys, probably aged three. It was the four of them in a seascape, she and her husband looking very happy together. Though the painting was from sixteen years ago, Lucy still looked the same, same hairstyle, same expression on her face. Her husband was strikingly good-looking. In the painting his eyes were a piercing light blue, his hair a blond-brown, cut short. His look was that of a cultured man with a rugged physique, a man who would look good wearing anything or nothing at all.

In the middle of the room was a white marble-topped coffee table flanked by ivory-colored sofas, one of which comfortably held Diana. She was wearing a denim skirt and jacket with a black turtleneck and black leggings. She had curled her long legs up informally on the formal sofa. Her black cowboy boots lay on the floor, next to a large casual-looking tan leather purse. As soon as she saw Eve, she sprang up as if she were a jack-in-the-box and bounded over to greet her.

"Eve! I was just telling Lucy we might have found our house. Jack and I discovered a lovely place on Rainbow Row. It was such an impulsive thing to do, but we put a contract on it."

Diana was excited as she gave Eve a little hug and returned to her spot on the sofa. Eve and Lucy followed, and shared the sofa opposite Diana.

"Tea, dear?" Lucy asked. "Unsweetened for you, of course."

"Yes, please," Eve said, "and after a day like today, I might like something stronger after lunch."

Eve caught herself and stopped before showing her emotions.

"Rainbow Row, you say?" she said.

On the coffee table were two glasses of iced tea and one empty glass, sitting next to two glass carafes. The larger one was half full, while the small carafe was filled to the top. Lucy used the small carafe to pour Eve her glass of unsweetened tea.

"Yes, it just went on the market," said Diana. "It's over two hundred and sixty years old and completely renovated. Everything's brand-new."

"How exciting," Eve said.

Though she was Diana's friend, Eve did feel a certain amount of jealousy. After all, Diana had not been born in Charleston.

"Isn't it, dear?" Lucy said. "It's not that common those houses go up for sale."

Lucy took a sip of her tea before getting up.

"Pardon me, ladies, but I need to step into the kitchen."

As she left the room, Diana looked at Eve and grinned. She pointed at her own leg.

"Can you believe she still wears pantyhose?"

"I know," Eve said in a whisper. "She so reminds me of her mother sometimes."

"Oh God, if that's not the kiss of middle age," Diana said. "I aspire to be nothing like my mother."

When Lucy returned she was carrying a large serving tray. The black lacquered tray held two glass serving platters trimmed in gold, a stack of small plates, forks, and folded napkins. One platter contained delicate cucumber sandwiches and quartered chicken salad sandwiches. On the other platter Lucy had carefully arranged deviled eggs and sweet pickles.

Lucy placed the black lacquered serving tray on the marble table, and passed the glass demi plates to her guests. The plates trimmed with gold had an Art Nouveau design on a burnt-pink background color. The centers of the plates were clear.

"At first I thought we should eat in the dining room, but since this is neither lunch nor supper, and given the circumstances of old friends, I thought a more relaxed setting was called for."

"Perfect," Diana said. "The more intimate the better."

Diana picked out two of each sandwich and two deviled eggs, and loaded her plate with pickles, while Eve placed one chicken salad sandwich and a pickle on her plate. Lucy, the ever-thoughtful hostess, chose one of each item after her guests had fixed their plates.

"Now, Lucy, that's your husband and kids over there, right?" Diana was pointing at the family painting on the wall.

"Yes, dear."

"He looks so familiar."

"And the painting doesn't do him justice," Eve said. "In person he looks like a tall Daniel Craig."

"Why thank you, dear, you are too kind," Lucy said. Her lips curled up with a smile of pride. "Theo's a good man and a loving father. The boys idolize him, he's the reason they both entered the Citadel."

"Eve said they're twins. What are their names?" Diana asked.

"Teddy and William," Lucy said. "Teddy's just like his father, but William has my heart. They are identical in every aspect except that one."

"And your husband, you had mentioned he was out of town?" Diana asked.

"Yes, dear. He's in Paris until the end of March. He comes home every other weekend or so."

"Gone for so long? Is his job military-based?"

"Oh no, he's employed with Hilton, in property development and management. There's a new hotel that's coming online, they're calling it the Hilton St.

Germain. He's there till they get the hotel open."

"You must miss him," Diana said.

"I do, very much, and with the boys in school we have the house to ourselves when he's in town. He's due back the week following this one."

"By your husband working in the hotel business, you must travel a lot."

"No, not so much anymore. When the boys were young, we traveled for vacations and such, but as Theo's career advanced, we traveled less and less. I've become a bit of a homebody." Lucy carefully wiped her mouth with her napkin to avoid smudging her lipstick. "When the market was hot in Paris, we even bought an apartment in the Champs-Élysées area. The company's European headquarters is based nearby, so he spends a great deal of time there."

"What about Folly?" Diana asked. "Do you go there often?"

"The old place has been closed up for about six years now. The last time we were out there was just after Momma passed away."

Lucy took a sip of tea.

"After Theo left the military and we moved back to Charleston, Momma gave this old house to us and she moved out to Folly. Since it was her family's place, she felt more comfortable at the beach house instead of here. I used to take the boys out there for the summers with Momma when Theo was out of town. Before she passed, she put the beach house in my name. Theo's been begging me to let him tear it down and develop the property."

"God, I loved that place," Diana said. "You're not going to sell it, I hope?"

"I'm indecisive about letting it go. It's the last

remaining parcel Momma's family owned. They moved there in the nineteen twenties, in fact, don't know if I ever told you two, but my mother's family owned the property around where DuBose Heyward lived and the place where George Gershwin stayed in thirty-four when he wrote *Porgy and Bess*. My great-uncle Joe used to go gambling and drinking with them."

When Lucy was finished with her story, Eve and Diana finished eating their light meal. Lucy took a few bites and set her plate down on the table.

"Would you all like a glass of wine? I've got a very nice old bottle of Château d'Yquem. Must be my family's Huguenot roots, but I do have a thing for good French wine."

"Oh yes, exactly what I need," Eve said with a little smile.

"Wine would be great," Diana said, "but that seems like such a lavish wine to open in the afternoon. Don't you want to save that for some special occasion?"

"This is a special occasion. We can toast to your new house and moving to Charleston."

"Okay, can't argue with that," Diana said.

Lucy gathered the plates, glasses, and carafes, placed them on the tray, and took them back to the kitchen. After she left the room, Diana quietly got Eve's attention.

"Eve, I think I got with him that first summer," Diana whispered. Her discomfited face contorted in a worried way.

"Who?" Eve asked.

"Her husband, Theodore. Please don't tell her."

"Oh God, Diana. Who did you not get with?"

"Oh come on, we were young then."

"I'm just saying, but don't worry, I won't say anything to her."

"Thank you."

When Lucy returned, she had a smaller serving tray. It was a round silver tray with a raised filigree edge. The tray held a bottle of wine, a corkscrew, and three clear big-bell red-wine glasses. She placed the tray on the table.

Lucy, in a very ladylike manner, deftly opened the bottle of wine and poured a small amount in the glasses. Picking up her glass, she swished the wine, taking in deep breaths before allowing any of the fragrant wine to reach her tongue. Her style was as expert as any sommelier's; she'd had much practice drinking wine by herself when her husband was away on business.

"Ah yes, that's very nice," Lucy said.

She asked them if they wanted a full glass. They all said yes and Lucy poured their glasses one by one. She sat back on the sofa with her glass. It was her ritual, her perfect joy.

Diana took a big sip of her wine and smiled.

"Very nice, Lucy," Diana said. "I'm wondering how you would both feel if we were to have something a little stronger."

"Whiskey?" asked Lucy.

"No. Something we did back in the summers on Folly Beach."

"I hope not beer," Eve said, "or certainly not that grog stuff Maggie made."

Diana said nothing. She reached down to the floor and grabbed her large leather purse. From within she pulled out a red silk box. The box was about eight inches long, two inches high, and four inches wide. The red silk looked very old and on top of the box was a golden dragon embroidered with gold metallic thread, adorned in a Chinese style. The front of the box had a tiny gold clasp shaped like a butterfly. Beneath it in gold thread were four Chinese characters.

Diana set the box down on the table and looked at her friends with a knowing smile. Lucy's curiosity was piqued, and she picked up the red dragon box. She looked at it from side to top and watched the golden dragon's thread throw off a little glimmer. The dragon's eyes had a hypnotic look and fire issued from its open mouth.

"Is it Chinese?" Lucy asked. "It looks very old."

"Is it a jewelry box?" Eve asked.

"No, not a jewelry box, and it is Chinese, and it's very old," Diana said. "When Jack and I were in China for a business trip, we got lost and we stepped into an antique shop for directions. No one could speak English, but I saw the box on the counter and had to have it. Our Chinese guide later told me it was an opium box from the early eighteen hundreds."

"An opium box? Really? My goodness, and such a pretty thing."

Lucy handed the box to Eve.

"Did your guide translate the Chinese characters on the front?"

"Yes, it's an ancient saying, 'Life is like a dream,' I think it was. He said that the box probably belonged to a woman, perhaps an aristocrat, or even a member of a ruling family. The gold thread is real gold."

Eve studied the box in detail.

"The butterfly is the clasp, I assume," she said.

"Yes, go ahead and open it," Diana said. "Just push down on it."

Eve gently pushed down on the butterfly clasp and the lid of the box popped up just enough to open. At once a heady herbal scent wafted out, one that Eve recognized but could not place. She opened the box until the hinged lid was upright. Inside she saw a small compartment filled with what she first thought were thin cigarettes. She then saw a small plastic bag tucked underneath. The bag bulged with marijuana.

"No. It isn't!" Eve said. "Are those joints in there?"

"Yes. I thought we should all go waltzing in Vienna." Diana grinned like the Cheshire cat and took another drink of her wine.

"Waltzing in Vienna. Now, that's an expression I haven't heard since our summers on Folly," Lucy said. "Do you still smoke marijuana, dear?"

"Yes."

"But now that you are older, aren't you concerned? You have a family and a successful business." Lucy's face expressed concern.

"Is it any worse than when my dad would drink three or four glasses of whiskey in the evening? Any worse than my mother taking Valium and other pills?" Diana coolly argued her point. "Don't you remember those summers at Folly? We were all getting high."

"But we were young, dear," Lucy said. "I did many things back then that I would never do now."

Eve was still holding the box and, her initial surprise having worn off, she placed it down on the table, directly in front of Diana. "From a clinical standpoint, marijuana is less harmful than cigarettes, with incidents of lung cancer and other health issues only a small fraction when compared to cigarette smokers. It's virtually nonaddictive, unlike the highly addictive nicotine in your cigarettes, caffeine in your coffee, and alcohol in your wine," Eve said. "Now there are over twenty states with legal medical marijuana laws, a dozen more with pending legislation, and of course recreational use legal in DC, Washington, Colorado, and now Alaska."

"There you go, Lucy, an endorsement from a professional."

"Well, perhaps not an endorsement, but I must say that I would like to try it again."

Eve looked furtively at the red dragon box. Diana picked up the box, opened it, and pulled out a joint and a lighter. "Come on, Lucy, let's smoke one."

"I'd like to," Eve said.

Always a gracious host, and despite her reservations, Lucy nodded her head. "Okay, but let me open a window."

Lucy stood up and walked over to the window by the fireplace. She pulled the sheers to the side, and after unlatching the ancient window she raised it up as high as it would go. Immediately a cool breeze from the bay slipped into the room. There was a freshness to the wind that livened up the room.

As soon as Lucy sat down, Diana placed the joint between her lips. With a roll of her thumb on the lighter, she produced a yellow flame. She touched the lighter to the tip of the joint and took a puff. The flame reached higher as it ignited the white paper tip. The smoke began to billow out, but disappeared as Diana took a deep drag. She held the smoke in her lungs and passed the lit joint to Eve, who plucked it with her thumb and index finger as if she were holding a single hair. Her little finger flared outward as if she were sipping tea from fine china. She slowly took a small puff, and then a deeper draw, only to cough the blue smoke back out.

Eve, still coughing, passed the joint to Lucy, but instead of holding it demurely as Eve had, Lucy placed it between her two fingers like a cigarette. She leaned back against the sofa and took a deep drag. This she held in her lungs like Diana, and for a moment she kept it in before exhaling. She placed the burning tip near her nose and took a deep breath before passing the joint back to Diana.

"That tastes very nice. It's a familiar earthy taste with notes of a green grassy flavor and a little floral undertone."

Lucy sounded as if she were giving wine tasting notes and the quip made Diana think there was more of Lucy's old self inside her than she let on.

Diana took another draw and passed it to Eve. This time Eve was able to inhale without coughing. The joint went back to Lucy and made another round before they finished it.

The air was thick with the pungent odor of the smoke while the three women sat still, quiet, until Eve erupted with laughter.

"Oh jeepers, I'm high!"

Eve's giggles made Diana and Lucy laugh.

"Lord, Diana, I do feel relaxed," Lucy said. "I'd forgotten how that actually feels. My senses being so alive too. The wine's even better, if that were possible." Lucy sniffed the bell of her wineglass and took a big sip. "So, tell me, how often do you smoke?" she said.

"On the weekends. Jack will have his cigar, and I'll smoke one or two. Every now and then I'll get high if I'm home and the kids are in school and he's at the shop. It's my time and beats the hell out of housework!"

"Oh you are too bad, Diana," Eve said. "Getting us started smoking pot again."

"Honey, if that's bad, then all of us were really bad in college. Besides, it wasn't Diana who got us started, it was Maggie...oh shucks! What was her last name?"

"Bloomer," Diana said. "Maggie Bloomer."

Eve was laughing. "The only thing more comical than her last name was that red hair of hers," she said.

"I had her old telephone number and called it yesterday," Diana said. "It was her mother's house in Mount Pleasant. She told me Maggie was living in Nepal and she gets a letter from her every once in a while."

"Nepal?" Lucy said. "Somebody at the church told me they saw her mother and she said she was in Peru. She was such a wild child. I remember the first time I met her, when you two pulled up at the beach house."

WALTZING in VIENNA

~4~

WALTZING IN VIENNA

Maggie Bloomer's pink Karmann Ghia coupe made its way down West Atlantic Avenue in the shabby-chic town of Folly Beach. Pink, the same shade as a Mary Kay Cadillac, was not the car's original color. Originally her father's car, the coupe had sat in the backyard of their house for four years after he passed away from cancer. For her sixteenth birthday, her mother had the car refurbished and painted pink, her favorite color. The car had become symbolic of her unique femininity, fierce independence, and connection to her father. It was more than a car. It was her statement to the world.

While the car's meager chrome bumper was too thin for bumper stickers, Maggie had arranged stickers to the right and left of the license tag. To the left, intentionally, was "Mike Dukakis for President" next to a "Question Reality" sticker. To the right was a green bumper sticker that read "Go Vegetarian" alongside a bumper sticker that read "Save Our Oceans." Just above the license tag was a round "Peace" sticker with an image of the earth behind it. Like her car, Maggie wore her heart on her sleeve.

From out of the open driver's window, Maggie's

long and curly red hair tossed in the wind. A pair of red heart-shaped Lolita sunglasses emphasized her decidedly heart-shaped face. Now twenty-one years old, she was a thin wisp of a girl, awash in pink and with an omnipresent personality.

In the passenger seat sat nineteen-year-old Diana Villiers, exuberant and fresh-faced. A pair of black Wayfarers sat atop her head, keeping her brown hair away from her face. She had finished her freshman year at the College of Charleston and she and Maggie were on their way to Lucy Bonneau's family beach house. Diana had come to know the Charleston socialite from a second-semester English class, and Lucy had invited her to the beach along with Lucy's childhood friend Eve Greene for summer break.

Maggie was Diana's suite-mate and a rising senior. She had become Diana's fast friend and was soon to become Lucy's unexpected guest.

On the radio Sinéad O'Connor's "Nothing Compares 2 U" played at full volume. Maggie was trying to tell Diana something, but her comment was washed away by the wave of sound. Diana could only see her lips move.

Diana turned the volume down. "What did you say?"

"It's Prince," Maggie said.

"What's Prince?"

"The song, Prince wrote it. The video is awesome too, she kind of reminds me of Joan of Arc with the shaved head."

"Yeah, that's cool."

Maggie turned the volume back up.

Diana was from Nashville, where her recently divorced parents were involved in the country music business. She had instantly liked the quirky Maggie, whose eclectic taste in music had fascinated her. Maggie style was nouveau hippie chic and her musical interests ranged from jazz and blues to the folk music of the nineteen sixties. In the conservative Southern environment of the College of Charleston, she stood out as a rebel, but anywhere else she would have been a normal alternative coed.

Before the song finished, Diana was pointing to the left side of the road at a pale-green house with white lattices.

"Here. Here. Turn here."

Maggie overshot the driveway and came to a stop in front of the house to the right of it. The yellow cottage was on stilts like all the other beach houses, and in the front yard were several eighteen- and nineteen-year-old boys playing football. Most were wearing familiar Citadel athletic shorts, and all of them were without shirts. They had short military-style hair and their sweaty chests glistened in the low-lying afternoon sun. One of the boys issued a hoot when he saw the two girls come to a stop, and they all stopped their game to size up Maggie and Diana. The boy who had hooted blew a kiss at them, and Diana cracked a smile. Her face flushed with the thought of how strong and virile they all looked. Maggie blew a kiss back to the boy and laughed aloud.

Her car made a little grunt as she backed up to the driveway of the light-green house. The beach cottage was on stilts too, with a wide set of white-trimmed steps in the front. To the left of the steps was a sign with the name "Maison de la Folie" burned in wood. The house was surrounded by windows with working storm shutters, and it looked old, but well cared for.

It was a classic low country beach house. At the head of the driveway was an older-model Mercedes silver sedan. On the right rear bumper was a "Bush-Quayle '88" bumper sticker.

Wax myrtles were scattered throughout the yard, punctuated by tall palmetto trees randomly placed by time and nature across a less-than-well-manicured lawn. Indeed, there were piles of palmetto fronds in various places in the yard. Two massive live oak trees anchored the left of the house to the earth. The trees wore gray gossamer dresses of Spanish moss that quivered at every breath of the wind. At the entrance of the driveway, an old mailbox stood as a solitary sentinel.

Beneath the house was a porch swing suspended from the bottom of the top level. Eve Greene sat there reading a well-worn book. She was wearing a navy blue one-piece bathing suit under a white silky blouse that was open in the front. Her hair was still damp from a swim in the ocean. Behind her and attached to the back of the house was a large deck off the first level. The deck had ancient gray steps that led down to a short wooden walk that snaked around a dune and ended on the beach.

As Maggie's car turned into the driveway and came to a rest behind the Mercedes, Eve put her book down and looked over at the pink car. Her squinted eyes opened up as soon as she recognized Diana in the passenger seat. She hopped up and walked over to the car just as Diana and Maggie were getting out.

"Hey! You found it."

Diana had a big smile on her face when she saw her friend Eve.

"Yes, and we got an eyeful of the neighbors,"

Diana said.

"Should be a fun summer. So many choices," Maggie said. She was laughing loudly.

"Oh, this is Maggie," Diana said, "the girl I've been telling you about." Diana nodded over to Eve. "Maggie, Eve Greene. She was in both semesters of English and in my psych 101 class."

"Pleased to meet you," Eve said.

"Yeah, you too," Maggie said.

Maggie took off her sunglasses to reveal pale-blue, almost lavender eyes. Her pastel eyes took Eve aback, and she could not help staring at her. The contrast of Maggie's red hair against her pale skin looked clownish, but her eyes were dazzling. She had a face that was both strikingly beautiful and slightly awkward.

Diana walked over to Eve and gave her a hug. Though Eve seemed to stiffen, Diana seemed not to notice and hugged her a little longer.

She took a good look around her and a deep breath of the sea air.

"Eve. It's so pretty here. I'm so excited."

"It's nice, isn't it? I've been coming here with Lucy since we were little kids," Eve said. "Just wait until you see the beach."

"Diana?" said a voice from the backyard.

From the back of the house, Lucy's vivacious face peeked around the corner. She waved hello.

"I'll be right there."

Maggie had already opened the hood of the Karmann Ghia, which was the trunk, since the engine was in the back. Diana's army surplus duffel bag came out first and Maggie placed it by her feet. Maggie's suitcase was a pink plaid, with a matching makeup case. She also pulled out a portable record player covered in pink vinyl and a white record case with painted pink flowers. By the time she had finished unloading the car, Lucy was there to greet them.

The young Lucy Bonneau was wearing lime-green-and-pink Lilly Pulitzer clamdiggers, flip-flops, and a sleeveless oversize pink cotton shirt. She had a figure that most women would love to have, an ample bosom with a small waist, but she hid it under a large shirt that shrouded her body. Her hairstyle and look was sixties retro without her intentionally trying to be.

"Oh Diana, dear, I'm so glad you made it." Lucy leaned over to Diana and gave her a friendly hug. She turned to Maggie. "Now, have we met?"

"No, I don't think so. I'm Maggie." Maggie reached for her hand and gave her a firm handshake.

"Lucy Bonneau. Pleased to meet you. But I've seen you before. Around school?"

"Maggie's at the college," Diana said. "She's my suite-mate."

"I'm a religious studies major," Maggie said. "Just one more year, and I'm done."

Maggie paused, almost humming as she looked around.

"I love your place," she said.

"Why thank you, dear. Mother's family has been here since folks started moving out here."

"Do you mind if I run my bags into the house?" Maggie asked.

"Go ahead, dear. The front door is always open."

Maggie grabbed her suitcases, tucked her record case under her arm, and headed for the house. Diana reached into the car and pulled out a small pink gift bag with a ribbon tied to the top.

"Here, I got you a little something for inviting us."

Lucy reached into the bag and pulled out a brown bamboo cup. Inside sat a green plastic straw and a paper umbrella swizzle stick.

"There's six cups. I thought they would be fun for drinks on the beach. Maggie also brought a bottle of rum. You know, she's legal."

"Oh, how nice, dear," Lucy said. She admired the gift. "I remember Momma and Daddy would make rum punch for their guests in something that looked just like that when I was a little girl."

"I hope you'll like Maggie. She's a great girl," Diana said. "It's okay she's here, right? You said I could bring a friend and she's the only one with a car who could take the time off."

"And what a car," Lucy said. "Of course it's okay."

Lucy watched Maggie as she walked back to the car, not knowing what to think of her. Maggie walked to the driver's side, opened the door, and carefully slipped her guitar from behind the driver's seat. The guitar was a small older Martin acoustic. Maggie had spray-painted it pink and had painted a reddish gerbera daisy on the tail of the guitar, just below the bridge. She walked over and picked up her record player.

"Okay, that's everything," Maggie said.

Diana picked up her bag and the women all went up the steps and into the house.

The house was a simple affair split into two sides. To the left was an open living area, and to the right were two bedrooms with a bathroom centered between them. The master bedroom was at the right rear of the house with its own bathroom and a large window that overlooked the beach.

To the left as they entered was an eat-in kitchen with pine-paneled cabinets. On the far left wall was the kitchen sink and above it a large window that stared directly at the neighbors' house. A bar with six stools running along the living area separated the kitchen from the back of the house.

The living room was a large open space, divided into two areas. In the center of the room was a loden love seat with two matching recliners that faced a small television set. An end table sat on each side of the love seat and between the recliners, and on top of each were hurricane lamps rigged with light bulbs. The light inside the milk glass cast a soft glow on the loden sofa and chairs.

A large leather sofa loomed in the rear of the living room. Years of use by friends and family in wet bathing suits had discolored and worn down the sofa's brown leather. Along the wall to the left sat an antique writing desk. Atop the desk was an older stereo system with a turntable and eight-track. A new compact disc player sat on top of the turntable lid.

In the left rear corner sat a bookshelf filled from top to bottom. Some of the books were ancient, and all of them had been read many times. There were modern dog-eared paperbacks alongside nineteenth- and twentieth- century classics by Dickens, Austen, Dumas, Verne, Wells, Joyce, and the Brontë sisters. A copy of Melville's *Moby-Dick* sat on the end table by the sofa. A reading lamp seemed to spotlight the book, as if it were in a bookstore display. The leather sofa could seat five adults and faced a large picture window that overlooked the beach and ocean. Just to the right of the picture window was a door that led onto the large sea-worn deck.

Paneled in heart of pine, the walls of the great room were dotted with family paintings and old photographs. Here and there were nautical things, a ship's wheel, panels of old maps, and photos of old boats. Long silky sheers draping the picture window along the back wall danced like synchronized swimmers in the sea breeze that slipped in through the open window. The floor was of more pine, with two old cable rugs, one in each half of the living area. If the house's furniture and decorations had all disappeared, it would have been a knotty symphony of pine.

"Cool place, Lucy!" Diana said. "This is your mom's?"

"Yes. Momma's family first moved out here back in the nineteen-thirties. Their first place got knocked down by Hurricane Gracie. In fact, the only thing that was still standing was that old deck in back. They kept the deck and rebuilt the house."

Maggie was looking at an old black-and-white photo hanging on the wall. In the picture was a portly man wearing dirty khakis, a white T-shirt, and a big straw hat. He was smoking a cigar and was standing by a massive pile of freshly caught fish spread out on the beach like tiny silver trophies. A group of young boys, most without shirts, stood around him, admiring his catch.

"Who's that?" Maggie asked. "He looks like W. C. Fields."

"That's my great-uncle Joe," Lucy said. "He owned a shop down on the original boardwalk, and had a big part in getting it built. He was part of Mother's family, my real uncle, you see, but everyone called him Uncle Joe. Everybody knew him and a lot of the old folks around here always told me he made his money from bootlegging and moved here to hide from the law. I don't really know, but he was quite the character."

"That's awesome," Maggie said.

She changed her first impression of Lucy. Maggie thought it was cool that her well-to-do family had such a skeleton in the closet.

"Well, girls," Eve said, "I'm going to go hop in the shower. See y'all in a bit." She put her paperback and sunglasses down on the kitchen bar and went into the bathroom.

"Diana, you and Maggie can take the center bedroom. There are two twins in there. I'm in the back and Eve's in the front bedroom. There are towels and sheets in the bathroom's linen closet."

"Thank you," Diana said.

"Yeah, thanks," Maggie said. "Let's go unpack, Di."

"I'm going to start supper in a bit," Lucy said. "I thought our first meal should be Frogmore stew. I'll be serving it on the back deck, on account of how messy it can get."

Diana scrunched her nose. "Frog stew? Never had frog before, but I'll try it."

Maggie and Lucy looked at each other, at first with coy smiles, then with light laughter. Diana was puzzled and wondered if she might be the butt of a joke.

"Come on, Di, I'll explain it to you while we unpack."

Diana and Maggie carried their bags into their bedroom as Lucy headed for the kitchen and began filling a great stockpot with water.

While unpacking, Maggie explained that Frogmore stew had nothing to do with frogs. It was a meal in one pot, a combination of smoked sausage, shrimp, red potatoes, and corn on the cob, all boiled together. It was a potluck dinner in one pot, and its strange name came from the community in the South Carolina Low Country where it had originated. It was also known as Beaufort boil and was an old-time dish for working folk.

When the girls had unpacked and refreshed themselves after the drive, they found Lucy in the kitchen draining all the steaming water out of the large pot. She asked Eve to grab the newspaper from the kitchen counter and go out back with her. She laid out the newspaper on the old round redwood table that sat on the back deck like a low-lying hill. Lucy dumped the pot out, and corn and smoked sausage rolled across the paper as if they were little barrels, surrounded by freshly cooked shrimp.

The four girls sat around with glasses of iced tea, except for Eve, who had a glass of ice water, and feasted on the dish, picking various things from the pile. Maggie, a vegetarian, ate only the potatoes and corn, while Eve ate a half dozen shrimp and two red potatoes. Lucy and Diana together ate the lion's share.

"Oh, I'm so stuffed," Diana said. "That was so much fun, eating outside. It's a pretty evening too. The sky's all pink."

To be sure, the sun was setting at the front side of the house, casting long shadows in the direction of the beach. From the deck, the horizon along the ocean was getting darker. Sun streaked in pink and crimson in long lines like waves in the sky. The colored fingertips faded to darker shades over the ocean. Diana's nose tingled from a hint of salt in the moist air, carried by a freshened breeze from the ocean. For a moment amid the conversation, the resonance of the sea breeze crept in. The ebb and flow of the wind caused the dry palmetto fronds, still hanging, to rustle and dance in the wind. Mixed in were the reverberations of wind chimes in the trees, some from their yard and others from their neighbors'. On top of this was the thud of the surf from the incoming tide. It was a quiet roar, and it completed the symphony.

"That's one of my favorite things to make," Lucy said. "Easy to prepare, and easy to clean up."

With that she took the newspaper that had served as a tablecloth and eating area and began rolling the edges to the center, making a bundle of the remains. She neatly took all of it away in one fell swoop.

"I'm going to run this downstairs to the trash can. Eve, you mind taking the stockpot into the kitchen?"

"Sure, Lucy, I've got it."

"When I get back I'll make us rum punch in those cute little cups."

Lucy carried the bundle down the steps of the deck as Eve took the big pot into the kitchen.

"Diana, I'm going to go get my cigarettes," Maggie said. "Do you think Lucy will mind?"

"I'm sure she'll be okay," Diana said.

Maggie disappeared through the door, leaving Diana to take it all in.

Diana thought about how wonderful it was to be

at the beach with her new friends. In high school she had not had many girlfriends. She'd preferred the company of boys, though she'd had only one boyfriend. He was on the baseball team, and it was a typical high school romance: dating, heavy petting, and then prom night, when she lost her virginity.

She saw him over the summer and he begged her to go to the University of Tennessee with him, but she did not like the idea of moving to Knoxville and eventually living together. More frightening than that was the thought that they would likely get married, have kids and a house, and end up like her parents. She wanted something different. She wanted to be her own person, so she chose the College of Charleston because it was small. It was near the beach, somewhere warmer, and farther away from her mother.

She adored her new friends. There were parts of all three women that she admired and wanted to learn more about. Maggie was a free spirit, and was extraordinarily bold with both women and men. There was an interesting juxtaposition within Eve. While she possessed a sweet naïveté, she was focused and intelligent. Most of all Diana admired Lucy, whom she saw as the older sister she'd never had. Despite the outward appearance of a Southern debutante, she was deeply astute and very wise. She was the most self-assured young woman Diana had ever met.

Her thoughts were interrupted by Maggie, who had returned with her pink record player and album box. She set the turntable up on the redwood table and flipped the lid open just as Eve returned. She uncoiled the power cord from the back of the record player and connected it to an outlet on the side of the house. After a few moments of flipping through her records, she found what she was looking for and placed it on the turntable. With a bump the needle hit the vinyl and Bessie Smith began belting out "Downhearted Blues."

"You know there's a CD player in there," Eve said.

"It's not the same," Maggie said. "There's something warm about an old record. Listen to her sing. That's a woman with real emotion, heartbreak and love, and joy and sadness, all at once."

Lucy carefully opened the door while carrying a large platter supporting the cups and rum punch.

"Well now, that's something a little older," Lucy said. "It sounds great."

The platter held four of the new bamboo cups, a pitcher of rum punch, fresh-cut limes, and the bottle of rum. She placed the platter on the table and began pouring the punch into the cups.

"Is there sugar in there?" Eve asked.

"Yes, dear."

"I can't have it."

"What about grog?" Maggie asked. "Here, let me show you, it's what sailors used to drink."

Maggie poured a shot of rum into one of the cups and picked up a few lime wedges. She squeezed the lime juice into the cup.

"Eve, pass me your glass of water, please."

Eve handed her the glass and Maggie poured some of the water into the cup. She stirred it and passed the stiff drink to Eve, who waited until Lucy had served up the rum punch to the other girls.

Lucy held up her cup. "Ladies, a toast. As my dear

mother always says, tchin-tchin."

Simultaneously they all raised their cups and toasted, saying, "Tchin-tchin."

"And what does that mean?" Diana asked.

"It's French, darling, means something like 'clink-clink.'"

With this they all toasted again and drank a second time.

"Oh my. This is sour." Eve pursed her lips together. "But I like it." She took a deep drink and finished her cup, surprising the other girls. "Maggie, another grog, please. My mother always told me, 'A drunk woman is not a pretty woman,' and I plan on testing that theory to see if it's true."

The girls all laughed along with Eve.

"Wow, I'm impressed!" Maggie said. She made Eve another cup of grog and passed it to her.

From a small bag, Maggie pulled out two cigarette cases. One was shiny sterling silver and the other had an enamel cover depicting mermaids beckoning sailors to the deep. They had long flowing hair and their arms were extended as they sang a siren song. She placed them on the table with a small sterling silver lighter.

"Lucy, do you mind if I smoke?"

"Only if you share." Lucy flashed a smile. "I'd love a cigarette. My mother's sister, Aunt Catherine, smokes, and she gave me my first cigarette when I was sixteen. Now, I'd never smoke in front of my momma. But Momma's not here."

Maggie opened up the sterling silver case and passed a cigarette to Lucy and then one to Diana.

"Eve? You want one?"

"Oh no. It's bad for your teeth."

"Eve's mother is a dentist," Lucy said, lighting up her cigarette. "She put the fear of God and tooth decay into her."

"That she did," Eve said. Eve's speech had become slurred and she spoke as if someone were holding the tip of her tongue. "But hey, I like this grog. There's no sugar so it's good for me. Can you make me another one?"

"Okay, one more," Maggie said.

As the evening turned to night, the girls drank their punch and smoked cigarettes, taking time to flip the Bessie Smith album.

"Hey, Maggie," Eve said. "I like this um...music. It's Messie Mith?"

Maggie burst out laughing and Diana began hooting. Lucy just had a big grin on her face.

"Eve, darling," Lucy said, "you've had six drinks to our three. Are you feeling all right?"

"Yes. Uh...no...I think I have to..."

Eve jumped up, ran for the edge of the deck railing, and threw up her dinner and her six drinks. She gagged and heaved a little more after returning to her seat.

"Oh, I'm seasick...uh. How did sailors drink grog and not get seasick?"

Eve jumped up again to throw up over the deck railing. This time it was only dry heaves.

"Honey, are you okay?" Lucy asked. The girls were laughing at Eve and her comments.

"Never been drunker, never been sicker."

Eve sat down and looked at her reflection in Maggie's sterling silver cigarette case. She put her hand to the side of her face and looked closer at her eyes in the silver reflection. "Looks like Mother was right! I'm not looking too pretty right now."

The three women burst out laughing. Lucy got up from the table. "Eve, sit still, I'll be right back."

She returned in a moment with a warm washcloth, a glass of water, and a couple of Tylenol. "Take these." Eve took the pills and started looking queasy again. Lucy passed her the washcloth. "Wipe your face with this and then press it over your eyes."

Lucy looked at Maggie and Diana and began to laugh.

"I'm cutting off the grog," Lucy said. She tried to look serious, but cracked up as Maggie and Diana laughed after her comment.

"Jeepers, I'm sick as a...a...a hog," Eve mumbled.

"You mean *sick as a dog*," Diana said.

"Yeah, a dog too," Eve said.

"Well, I do have something that will make you feel better," Maggie said.

"You do-do," Eve slurred. She pulled the washcloth away from her face. Her eyes were red and puffy.

"Yes. Well, it's not exactly legal."

"What is it, dear?" Lucy asked.

"Pot."

"I'm sorry?"

"Mary Jane, you know, marijuana. I have some joints rolled."

Lucy looked appalled. "Oh no, no, no. That's so illegal. You brought pot into my parents' house. Diana, did you know that?"

"No, I didn't." Diana flashed a nervous "What?" look at Maggie.

"But we are underage and drinking alcohol," Maggie said.

"She does have a point, Lucy," Diana said.

"Well yes, I realize that. But is it safe? It's an illegal drug, for goodness' sakes. Alcohol is legal, though we may not be. Anyways, you always hear about people getting addicted to marijuana, and then it leads to hard drugs."

Maggie and Diana grew quiet. There was a pause for a few seconds, a moment of hush that seemed to last for an hour.

"Wait a minute, Lucy," Eve said. Her head was bobbing around in a drunken swirl. "In psych class I remember reading that nicotine and caffeine is more additive than the stuff in pot."

"You mean addictive, dear," Lucy said. "Still, it makes me very nervous to have it in the house. What if someone smells it and calls the law?"

Maggie looked down at the table while a sad feeling of discouragement washed over her face. Up until this point, she had let her flag fly and her new friends had accepted her. As the evening had gone on she had become more comfortable, but now that comfort was broken.

"Lucy, I'm sorry I brought it. I'll leave if you want."

The issue had now become a conundrum for Lucy. Though she felt uncomfortable with the marijuana in her parents' house, the hostess in her did not want to offend her guest. This was in addition to the feelings of adventure inside of her. She wanted to live life and experience new things. It was a feeling of conflict that she had felt before as a young girl in her parents' world, doing the things she was supposed to do instead of what she wanted to do.

Lucy relented. "Honey, there's no need for that.

Are you sure it's safe?"

"Bessie Smith smoked it," Maggie said. "So did Margaret Mead and Lillian Hellman. I'll tell you who else smoked pot, Louisa May Alcott."

"Didn't she write *Pretty Woman?*" Eve said. "Then if I smoke it, will I be pretty again?"

The serious look on Lucy's face faded and she began to laugh. "Sweetie, she wrote *Little Women. Pretty Woman* was a movie with Julia Roberts."

There was laughter from the other two girls, causing the heavy mood to drift away.

"I'll try it," Diana said. "Come on, Lucy. I don't think anyone's going to smell it with this breeze."

Lucy caved in. "Okay. If Alcott smoked it and it will help my friend be prettier, then let's do it."

Maggie opened up the mermaid cigarette case. Inside were a dozen neatly arranged joints. She pulled out one and held it up for them to see.

"Since y'all have never tried it, let me tell you. We share it and pass it around, and when you take the smoke in, hold it for as long as you can. Okay?'

Maggie placed the joint between her pink lips and picked up her silver lighter. When she clicked the lighter, the flame danced around the tip of the joint. She inhaled deeply and passed it to Diana.

"Here, now you take a hit and pass it to Lucy."

Diana took a deep drag. She gasped to get the smoke into her lungs. It felt warm, with a spiciness that she had never tasted. It was better than the cigarette, and had a green and earthy flavor. She passed it to Lucy, who took a deep drag before passing it on to Eve, who took the joint and pinched it with her thumb and middle finger. Eve took a deep drag and immediately coughed it back out. She passed it back to Maggie.

The joint went around again before Maggie lit up a second joint and passed it around as well. The four girls began to feel the effects and they went from being intoxicated to being stoned. It was an easier feeling for them, relaxed, and for the first time since getting drunk Eve did not look so queasy.

"Jeepers, I feel better," Eve said. Her voice was melodic and she began to sing. "'Jeepers creepers, where'd you get them peepers? Jeepers creepers, where'd you get them eyes?'"

Eve's voice trailed down in volume but she was still singing the words to herself. Diana was watching the performance and laughing.

"This is better than I expected," Lucy said. "It's calmer. I thought I'd feel nervous, but this feels good, like a warm bath."

Lucy stopped talking and watched Eve's head sway from side to side as she sang at the top of her voice.

"Sweetheart, I like Louis Armstrong as much as anyone, and no offense, but I don't believe you do that song any justice."

Diana laughed hysterically.

"Here, let me put on another album," Maggie said.

Maggie picked up the Bessie Smith record that had been going around in circles with a rhythmic click. It had long ended. She slipped it into its sleeve and then produced another shiny black album out of her record box. With deft skill she placed the needle on the disk and started Joni Mitchell's "Help Me."

Maggie stood up and started dancing to the song around the table and the open deck. She danced with a slow hippy sway, occasionally turning with her long red hair spinning like a top. By now the moon had risen over the shoreline. It was dark, and the silvery rays made Maggie's dance look ethereal.

As the other women watched, Eve giggled; though she did not know the song, she was singing, "Help me" during the choruses. Diana and Lucy looked on, occasionally smiling at one another. Maggie's dance both amused them and heightened their sense of mischievous delight in being high.

As the song went on, Lucy looked deep in thought. Maggie was in her world and Eve was staring off into space.

"With the standards of how women were in her day, it's no wonder Alcott smoked pot," Lucy said.

"I read *Little Women* in high school. It was kind of boring to me," Diana said.

"I agree. I think a lot of people nowadays would say so." Lucy lit up a cigarette she had pulled from Maggie's silver case. "Did you know she wrote it to please her daddy? Though she enjoyed the success from it, she disliked it, even called it 'moral pap for children.' Alcott was definitely not a 'little woman.' No, I really believe she would have preferred to write stories about women like Chopin's Edna in *The Awakening*."

"You mean Kate Chopin?" Diana asked.

"Yes. That book made me consider what some women become and what others try to run from. Edna is such a complex character, full of passion and desire, yet stuck in a time and place that forced her to be so reserved and restrained. Edna is a little like Icarus. Do you know the story of Icarus?"

"No, but the name sounds familiar."

"It's a Greek myth. Icarus was a young man imprisoned on the island of Crete along with his father. Surrounded by water, they planned to escape using wings he and his father made from feathers and wax. Before they flew away, his daddy told him, don't fly too close to the sun, since the wax would melt. But once Icarus started flying, the joy of being free overcame him and he flew higher and higher until the wax melted and his wings fell apart. He plunged into the sea and drowned."

"Oh my," Diana said.

"Do you see the connection? Edna flew too close to the sun, too close to her passions. In the end, after she's destroyed emotionally, she goes for a swim in the ocean and lets the water overcome her and drowns."

"I know you're an English lit major, but you have a real passion for this stuff."

"Every time I saw my aunt Catherine, she would give me a new book to read and we'd talk about it the next time I saw her. I remember the first volume she gave me. It was Emily Brontë's *Wuthering Heights*. I loved the language, the way she wrote, and the idea of writing for the heart of a woman, it thrilled me. One of the last books she gave me was Virginia Woolf's *A Room of One's Own*. Have you ever read it?"

"No."

"It's more of an essay than anything. The whole idea being, as Woolf says, 'A woman must have money and a room of her own to write fiction.' After college, I want to go to Europe, visit the old cities, and tour the countryside. Then I'd go live in Paris and write about my experiences. The thought of it sounds so free and filled with limitless possibilities."

"Limitless possibilities. I like the way that sounds. It's one of the reasons I moved to Charleston to go to school. My parents dated in high school and after they graduated from the same college, they got married. Can you imagine only being with the same guy? Sex with the same guy? What's really bad about it is my parents just got divorced after my mom caught him cheating on her."

"I'm sorry to hear that, dear, sorry for your mother and what she went through. It's got to be a hard thing to suffer betrayal like that after you've known someone for so long."

No one had noticed, not even Maggie, for she was still dancing, that the Joni Mitchell record had ended. It was still spinning and there was the rhythmic click-click-click of the needle as it slid into the center of the shiny black vinyl record. The infinite revolutions held Eve's stoned attention.

"Maggie, you do realize that there's no music playing?" Lucy's comment ended Maggie's trancelike dance.

"Huh? Oh, I got lost in the dance. God I love to dance when I'm stoned."

Maggie walked over to the record player, moved the arm over to the resting position, and broke Eve from her stoned daze. It brought everyone's attention to Maggie.

"I want to learn how to waltz. Teach me, Lucy. You must know how. I saw a picture of you in a debutante gown in the house. Where did you debut?"

"The St. Cecilia Society, and yes, I've danced a waltz or two."

Maggie walked over to Lucy and held her hand out. "Will you do me the honor?" Maggie asked.

"Oh, if I must," Lucy said. "Pardon me, Diana; Maggie's name is next on my dance card."

Lucy stood up and accepted Maggie's hand. "So, I will be lead and you will follow. Stick your right arm out and your hand in mine, your left arm goes here."

"Are you dancing Viennese style?" Eve asked.

"Yes, dear, the dance originated in Vienna. There are three beats to the bar and we will dance natural, so we will turn to my right, clockwise, as we traverse the deck counterclockwise. I will count them as we go." Lucy stood tall and held her hands out. "Are you ready?"

Maggie nodded and stepped up to her, taking her hand. With Lucy taking the lead the two moved clockwise in a waltzing motion as she counted.

"One-two-three, one-two-three…"

"This is fun, Lucy, I feel like we are floating," Maggie said. "Like we are waltzing in Vienna." She began to sing to Lucy's counting. "Waltzing in Vienna, waltzing in Vienna, you'll come a-waltzing in Vienna with me."

Diana and Eve watched their silhouettes dance across the deck under the silver moonlight. They all began to sing along with Maggie.

"Waltzing in Vienna, Waltzing in Vienna, you'll come a-waltzing in Vienna with me."

The sound of their singing and the echo of the crashing surf made their dance more wraith-like than a waltz. They were floating in the night's seaborne air like spindrift on the water's surface. It was a moment they would always remember, under the magical open space of the sky and the stars.

WALTZING in VIENNA

~5~

HARRISON AND PORTER

O ver the following days, the girls bonded under the freedom that came from the absence of parents or chaperones. With work, school, and schedule stripped away there was a freedom from all defining things, and it allowed them to let down their guard and put aside their differences. They soon abandoned the confines of what they may have thought of one another on campus, realizing that basically, they were all the same.

They shared stories about their pasts, about boyfriends they wished they had and boys they wished they had never met. Within their unlikely camaraderie, they discussed their present station and called for a total rejection of what they believed their parents wanted from them. It was both rebellious and exciting for them to consider themselves fiercely independent women who spoke their minds. While the four girls had different aspirations for their future, they all saw themselves making their way as the modern women they imagined.

Each long and languid day began with Diana waking up at six o'clock to make a pot of coffee. She was always the last to go to bed and the first to rise, and she would start her day with a cup of coffee on the back deck paired with a couple of Maggie's long menthol cigarettes. With regularity she would watch a few of the cadets next door go out for a morning run down the long beach wearing nothing but boxer shorts. Each morning Diana was there, watching their young and lean bodies take their long strides, their feet pounding across the sand.

There was a side to Diana that required solitude and she would go outside with her coffee and share a cigarette with the rising sun. There was also a side of Diana that loved to look at men and the physicality of their muscles and body shape. She loved the male form, a broad chest, the curve of the biceps, and a taut rear end. The feeling she got from watching them run, if only for a moment, stimulated her more than a dozen cups of coffee.

When the silhouettes of the cadets disappeared along the line of the beach, Diana would go back inside and find Eve sitting at the kitchen counter flipping through one of the psychology journals she had borrowed from school. Eventually Lucy and Maggie would roll out of bed, and *breakfast* usually meant a bowl of cereal or yogurt. Sometimes it meant just coffee.

Following breakfast they welcomed the warm sun, lying out on beach towels, in Maggie's case under the beach umbrella. Lucy and Diana would talk about books and women writers while Maggie listened in. Eve on the other hand would don her swim cap and goggles and go for lengthy swims in the ocean. While Eve may have been awkward in conversation, her long graceful body cut through the water with speed and precision. Behind Lucy's house the beach was not as crowded as behind other houses on Folly. Save for a beachcomber looking for sharks' teeth or people walking their dogs, few passed by.

Occasionally a stray football would fly into their area of the beach, "accidentally" thrown out of bounds by one of the Citadel boys next door. Usually the ball would fall near where they were lying, and the boys would take turns going over to retrieve the ball and beg their pardon. Whoever the boy, he would get his closer look, run back over to his own yard, and make his report. The girls could just barely hear the boys talking about them.

When the afternoon shadows stretched across the beach, they would return to the house and get ready for the evening. Dinner was always a sumptuous affair and Lucy would serve up the kind of large Southern meals she had learned from her mother how to make. Inspired by the fresh seafood caught by the local fishermen, the girls enjoyed fried flounder, shrimp étouffée, and crab cakes. Other times it was fried chicken or barbecued ribs, and sometimes a Continental offering such as beef bourguignonne. Every dinner included a plethora of vegetables and side dishes and was spread out on the big redwood table on the back deck just as dusk rolled in with the ocean tide. Afterward Lucy would make rum punch, and though Eve no longer had a taste for grog, she drank herbal tea as she and the others listened to Maggie's collection of folk music and old blues albums. There was also much waltzing in Vienna under the moon and summer stars.

It was the Saturday after Maggie and Diana had arrived. As on every morning, Diana was sitting on the steps of the immense deck smoking her cigarette, with a mug of coffee by her side. Her eyes were following four jogging cadets as they ran down to the beach when she heard the roar of a motorcycle. The sound was the unmuffled and uniquely skipping pop-pop sound of a Harley-Davidson motorcycle. Lucy's was always a quiet neighborhood, and after all, it was six thirty in the morning. Diana was so startled she dropped her cigarette and darted into the house. The noise had already woken Lucy, who was making her way to the kitchen in her long cotton nightgown.

Lucy had to raise her voice over the roar of the motorcycle.

"What on God's green earth is that?"

"Don't know," Diana said. "I was out back when I heard it. It's coming from the neighbor's house."

Lucy reached the kitchen sink that overlooked the neighbor's yard. She was pulling the curtains to one side as Maggie sleepily came out of the bedroom wearing pink Betty Boop pajamas.

"What's going on?" Maggie asked.

Lucy was staring out the window.

"Some boy on a motorcycle is pulling in at the Taylors' house next door."

"Oh, let me see," Diana said.

She took a quick step to the kitchen window.

"That sounds like a Harley," Maggie said.

"Harley? Oh no, that's a man," Diana said, "and what a beautiful-looking man he is too."

Maggie slipped between Lucy and Diana, sharing

the beautiful view through the window.

The three girls watched the stranger's bike go rolling under the neighbors' house. His wavy blond hair cascaded from beneath his helmet, and when he removed the helmet they watched him run his fingers through his hair. He was wearing a black T-shirt under a black leather jacket, and his tight blue jeans were made tighter because he was straddling his motorcycle. He sat for a moment, removed his sunglasses, and looked at the time on his wristwatch. Arching his back, he stretched his muscular arms out before shutting off his motorcycle.

Eve was the last to wake up and she came out of her room wearing men's blue flannel pajamas.

"Good morning. What was all of that noise?"

"We have a new neighbor," Diana said.

"The Taylors? I thought they went up to Maine for the summer."

"No, dear, some boy on a motorcycle," Lucy said.

"Really? Is he a cute boy?"

"He's a real man, no boy there," Diana said.

"Well, if you like that kind of thing," Lucy said. "He's in serious need of a shave and haircut."

"And Lucy's just the woman to do that," Diana chuckled.

Lucy's round cheeks went scarlet.

"Oh honey, he's not my type."

Eve moved closer and all four girls were staring out the window. They watched him remove the bungee cords from his duffel bag and lift the heavy sack over his shoulder. He fished a shiny gold key from his pocket and carried his bag up the steps to the front of the house. After unlocking the door, he let himself in.

Eve, who was no longer staring out the window, poured herself a glass of orange juice and sat down at the long bar overlooking the kitchen. Diana freshened her coffee and sat down next to Eve while Maggie was in the refrigerator pulling out an apple. Lucy was still hanging over the sink looking out the window.

"I wonder who he is," Eve said. "He looked suspicious. Do you think he looked suspicious? Do you think you should go talk to him, Lucy?"

"Talk to him? Oh no…no need. He's probably renting the place from Mr. Taylor. They've rented it out before."

When Lucy realized she was the only one standing by the sink, she closed the curtain and began rinsing out a coffee mug, as if that were the real reason she was there.

"Come on, Lucy, you know you want to go talk to him," Diana said. "If you don't go, I might."

Lucy poured herself a cup of coffee and walked over to the bar, where the other girls sat chatting about the stranger next door.

"A man like that only wants one thing," Lucy said. "You know there'll be a revolving door of girlfriends over there. I want a man who's refined and well-read, someone who wants the same type of life I want. Not some long-haired grease monkey."

"I don't believe you, Lucy," Diana said. "I saw you staring at him."

"No interest here," Lucy said.

Diana smirked at her. "Whatever you say. I'm going to go have a cigarette. Anyone want to join me?"

"I'll be right there, Di," Maggie said. "Let me put on a pair of jeans and grab my cigarettes." Maggie ducked into the bedroom.

Eve finished her orange juice with a short chug.

"I'll pass. Think I may go for a swim."

"And I'm going back to bed," Lucy said. "You all wake up too early for this woman."

Lucy took her unfinished coffee into the kitchen and headed back to her room, but not before peeking out the kitchen window one last time. Diana was the only one who saw it. Lucy's crush on the man on the motorcycle delighted her.

It was not long before Eve came out of the house. She was wearing her navy blue one-piece and was carrying her swim goggles and cap. Diana was sitting at the redwood table cupping her coffee between her hands.

"That water's going to be cold this early in the morning," Diana said.

"It's okay, I take cold showers too. It's better for circulation and improves lymphatic movement."

Eve bounded down the steps and over the boardwalk path to the beach. Diana watched her don her swim cap and make her way down to the beach, easing herself into the water before jumping a wave and swimming out past the wave break. Diana watched her long arms dig into the water, propelling her in a long line along the shore. She was mesmerized watching Eve's embrace of the water until Maggie appeared on the deck and the door behind her snapped closed. She was wearing blue jeans and a pink paisley shirt that resembled an old pajama top. The well-washed shirt softened Maggie's pointy features. Maggie had her pink acoustic guitar in one hand and her cigarettes in the other. A capo topped with a butterfly was clipped on the fourth fret.

"Hey, great! You got your guitar."

"You did so well yesterday with the chords I showed you, so I thought I'd teach you a real easy song."

"What's the song?"

"'Jolene' by Dolly Parton. Do you know it?"

"Of course I do, my mom worked as a secretary at RCA before I was born."

"Oh wow. You never told me that, Di."

"It was for a couple of years before she quit to go work with my father."

"So you know the song. Great. Let's start with the chorus. It's A minor." Maggie strummed the chord. "Then change to C by moving your ring finger up; then G, you remember that one, and back to A minor." She repeated the chord progression. "That's the first line. The second line is the G, and then end with the A minor, and then repeat it all. Okay? So, here it goes. Watch my fingers."

Maggie sat up straight and cleared her throat. She took a deep breath and played a little intro before starting the chorus. She sang out strong and clear, her voice summoning a pleading cry across a jingle-jangle rhythm, like Dolly Parton's.

Diana enjoyed Maggie's rendition of the song, and for her it reinforced the emotional power of music. She thought of how powerful one could be with just a guitar, a voice, and heartfelt lyrics. Not only was it a beautiful song, but it was a sad pitiful plea, the singer begging Jolene to leave her man alone, rather than fighting for him.

"Okay, now you try." Maggie passed the guitar to Diana. "Before you start, play each chord to get your fingers used to it."

Diana put the guitar across her knee and wrapped her arm around the body. She carefully placed her hand on the neck of the guitar and fretted the chords, strumming each one.

"Okay, now try to sing it as you play. Don't be afraid, just let the chords melt into the words and let your voice join the tone of the guitar."

"Wait. Don't you think the woman would be angry at Jolene?" Diana asked. "I know you sang it the right way, but if I was her, I'd be angry."

"Well, yeah, good point. The thing about music is there is no right way. You should sing it the way it feels to you."

"I'm ready."

Diana paused for a moment and nervously took a deep breath. She played the first chord with a hard downstroke and punched the first word, "Jolene." An angry "Jolene" followed each forceful chord. She sang the rest of the chorus slowly, deliberately, and angrily.

"Jolene should be worried," Lucy said. She had been standing in the back doorway the whole time Diana was giving her interpretation of the song.

"Damn, Di, that was badass," Maggie said.

The power in Diana's voice impressed her, and added another unexpected layer of coolness to her friend.

"You-all have an audience," Lucy said. "Our new neighbor's listening in."

Lucy nodded her head over to the lot next door and grinned at them. Maggie and Diana looked over and through the trees. The long limbs of the live oak tree opened just enough for them to see the stranger next door sitting on the small back porch. They could see his broad chest and thick arms wrapped tightly beneath his black T-shirt. He had a cigarette dangling from his mouth, and as soon as the girls turned around, he gave a little friendly applause. Though he was too far away to have heard anything, he nodded his head and smiled at them.

Diana laughed and grinned at Lucy. "He's smiling at you, Lucy."

"Yeah, right," Lucy said. "I bet you that man will smile at any girl who gives him the time of day. I'm going to put some biscuits in the oven and open a jar of my mother's peach preserves. Y'all come on in after you've knocked old Jolene around a bit."

Lucy laughed at her own joke and went back into the house while Maggie walked Diana through the rest of the song.

As soon as the scent of biscuits was in the air, they gave the song a rest and went inside to the warm kitchen. Diana noticed someone had pulled the curtain over the sink to the side, leaving the view open wide. She said nothing to Lucy, but watched her every now and then glance out the window.

The three girls sat at the kitchen bar eating the warm biscuits with butter and the sweet preserves. They each had coffee and got into a discussion about what they would do if Jolene tried to take their man. Their conversation quickly moved into the ridiculous, punctuated with laughter. Lucy said she would make Jolene eat until she was fat, Maggie said she would shave off her "auburn hair," and Diana plainly said she would kick her ass. The girls were still laughing at Diana's frankness when there was a knock on the door.

"I wonder who that is," Lucy said. "It's still early."

Maggie started laughing and looked at Diana. "Is it

the motorcycle man?"

Diana laughed too. Lucy rolled her eyes and walked to the front door. She looked through the peephole and turned around to the girls. "Now, this is strange," she said.

With that she turned the deadbolt lock and opened the door. Standing on the threshold was Porter Hayes, a professor of English at the College of Charleston. Indeed, it was in his very class that Eve and Lucy had first met Diana. He had just turned thirty-nine years old and was quite handsome and a slight man physically. His well-coifed hair, piercing blue eyes, and sharp features made him look more like an Englishman than a Charleston-bred American. He was wearing seersucker pants, suede saddle shoes, a crisp blue oxford shirt, and a red bow tie. A small briefcase was hanging from his left hand.

"Good morning, Miss Bonneau."

"Dr. Hayes. Good morning to you. What a surprise to see you here at Folly."

"Miss Bonneau, I apologize for the imposition during your summer break. I was hoping I might find Miss Greene. I saw your mother at the Lyric Opera Society last night and she told me you both were here and gave me the address."

"It's quite all right. Do come in."

"Hi, Professor Hayes," Diana said.

"Miss Villiers, what a pleasant surprise. I had no idea you were here as well." Professor Hayes looked over at Maggie and nodded his head. "Miss Bloomer."

"Hi, Professor." Maggie smiled a little as she tried to keep a straight face.

There was a moment of awkward silence as the

professor stood there. Though eloquent when he spoke in class, he was reserved in private conversation, especially with women. He curiously looked around the beach house. On the wall opposite the kitchen, beside the bedroom doors, hung a picture of the old Folly Beach pier, long since washed away by a hurricane.

"Well, look at that. The old pier. I remember sitting on the benches watching the fishermen when I was a little boy. After my father passed away, mother and I would come down and visit with my aunt Tessie."

"My mother has fond memories of that old pier too," Lucy said. "Dr. Hayes, you said you wanted to see Eve?"

"Yes. I drove down to have a word with Ms. Greene. I realize it's early. I'm more of a morning person. Early to bed, early to rise for me." He babbled on. "Is she here…I mean available?"

Lucy was watching the professor with her hands on her hips. She was curious as to why he had made the thirty-minute drive from Charleston so early in the morning just to see one of his students. As he spoke to her with his back turned to the others, she saw Maggie whisper something in Diana's ear. Both girls were smiling, trying not to laugh.

"Eve went out for a morning swim about a half hour ago. She should be back anytime now."

Lucy offered him coffee and biscuits. He declined both. Instead he stood in the same spot and nervously looked at the pictures on the wall. The three girls were perplexed as to what to do next. It was a discomfiting moment. They lost their stride of their conversation and the silence of Professor Hayes was deafening.

In whispered voices Maggie and Diana picked back up on their discussion about music and the virtueless Jolene, while Lucy quietly cleaned the kitchen. All three girls waited with a curious fascination for Eve to return, wondering why a college professor would visit a student during the summer break.

After what seemed like forever, but was actually only a few minutes, Eve Greene came in through the back door with a look of relaxation on her typically ill-at-ease face. Her lithe body was more toned than ever after her morning swim and there was confidence in her step.

"Oh!"

Eve panicked at the thought of the professor seeing her in her bathing suit. She saw him pointing to a photograph on the wall and asking Lucy if that was her aunt Catherine. For an instant she was frozen in her pose like a statue covered by morning dew. Her only movement was the mortified glaze that filled her eyes and the blush of embarrassment that rolled across her cheeks.

Professor Hayes turned to see Eve standing by the door. "Well, Miss Greene. There you are."

She jerked out of her frozen stare and grabbed the closest thing she could find to wrap around her. It was a well-worn but charming wool blanket with two gardenias in the center. In the process of fixing her impromptu shroud, she dropped her swim goggles and cap. While she was nervously running her fingers through her hair, the professor walked over to her and bent down to pick up the items she had dropped.

"Miss Greene, you dropped these." He nervously

offered the items back to her.

In a shy, hushed voice, she replied to him. "Thank you."

"You are certainly welcome."

There was another awkward pause. The other girls were watching Eve and the professor, not knowing what to do or say. Finally Lucy piped up. "Eve, dear, the professor came out to see you."

"Yes, I have some school-related business that I need to speak to you about."

"School-related?" Eve asked.

"Professor," Lucy said, "perhaps if you give Eve a moment to dress, you two could have a little privacy on the back deck."

"Yes, of course," he said. "Perhaps I will have that cup of coffee after all."

"Come on, Professor, let's go get you a cup while Eve takes a moment."

Lucy smiled and nodded to Eve. She made a short run for her bedroom. When she returned, the girls noticed that she had slipped on a pale-blue cotton shift. For the past week she had been either in her bathing suit or in shorts; the choice of clothing was curious to say the least. She had also taken the time to brush out her hair.

Eve furtively looked around the house and asked just where Professor Hayes was. Lucy pointed to the back door and Eve could see the professor sitting on a bench on the back deck drinking his coffee. There was a little caution in her walk to the back door, but she managed to go out and sit with Professor Hayes without tripping or looking clumsy.

Lucy watched Maggie and Diana stare through the back door window and walked over to them for the same vantage point.

"Oh my. I do wonder what that's all about," Lucy said.

During the whole of the professor's visit, Maggie and Diana had been whispering to one another, occasionally swallowing down a giggle or two. Now they watched him pull out a fistful of papers from his briefcase, showing them to Eve and pointing to the pages with his index finger. They saw her smile and mouth, "Thank you."

When Porter and Eve finished their meeting, they walked back into the house. The smiles on their faces showed like bright streaks of sunlight on a cloudy day. A connection had been established, and it was clear there was chemistry between them. Their meeting had begun clumsily, like an ill-fitting garment, but now they looked like a pair of matched soft shoes. Eve walked him to the door, gave him a big smile, and said her good-bye. He smiled back at her and reached to hold her hand, kissing it in the formal European way. Porter nodded to the rest of the girls and told them "good day" before walking out the door.

When the door snapped shut, Eve covered her mouth with both hands. "Oh my God!"

"What is it, dear?" Lucy asked.

"Yes, tell us," Maggie said.

"He came to tell me Dr. Scott, my psychology professor, is recommending a paper I wrote for the *American Journal of Relational Psychology*. Dr. Hayes is going to edit it for me. Can you believe that? He said Dr. Scott told him it would be the first time a college freshman had a paper published in that journal."

"So why didn't Dr. Scott come out and tell you the news?" Diana asked.

"Because Porter"—Eve paused—"I mean Dr. Hayes, is going to help me to get it ready to meet the July fifteenth deadline. He's coming back next Thursday and taking me to the Crab Shack at six to go over the markup. He's taking care of dinner too."

"Darling, that sounds like a date," Lucy said.

"Sounds like that to me too," Maggie added.

"Oh no, it's strictly professional."

"If you say so," Diana said.

Maggie had a little devilish smile on her face. As soon as she looked at Diana, they burst out laughing.

"Oh stop it, y'all. He's twice my age, and he's my professor."

"But he is a man," Diana said.

"Now, leave Eve alone," Lucy said. Her straight face turned to a smirk. "I think the idea of her having an older gentleman caller is just charming."

Maggie and Diana burst out laughing. Lucy was laughing so hard tears were running down her face.

"I'm sorry Eve. You know I'm just funning with you," Lucy said.

"It's okay, Lucy."

WALTZING in VIENNA

6~

BOYS OF FOLLY BEACH

"Listen y'all," Lucy said, "I want to make some she-crab soup tonight with red ricc and green beans and there's a place off the beach that always has blue crab. I want to take a drive out there and pick up some and a get a little produce. Why don't we all go and on the way stop at the pier and do a little shopping?"

"Yeah. We need more rum and I need to get more cigarettes," Maggie said. "What about you, Di?"

"Okay, it will be fun to get out. I'm up for it."

"Me too," Eve said.

The girls disappeared to dress for the day and ready their faces and hair. Eve emerged wearing a pair of long khaki shorts and a pink polo top. She flipped the collar up and threw on a pair of oversize sunglasses. Maggie and Diana were in shorts as well, but theirs were much shorter than Eve's "mom" shorts. A white cotton button-up shirt finished Diana casual look, while Maggie wore a black Roy Orbison concert T-shirt. The three of them stepped outside to wait for Lucy.

Diana spotted him first. The stranger next door was sitting down on the concrete slab beneath the house. He had the spark plug wires pulled from the engine of his motorcycle, and he was opening a box of new spark plugs. The other girls joined Diana in watching him. Peering down from the front deck, they could see him crouched down in his blue jeans. A black T-shirt was hanging from the handlebars of his bike. His back was turned and he could not see them studying him, watching his every move. Diana's eyes followed the curve of his back as he leaned over. It was as if it were a road map to a place where she wanted to go. She liked the way his long blond hair draped down over his strong shoulders.

Lucy stepped out of the house looking ready for a summer day. She was wearing a cute flower-print wrap skirt and an oversize purple polo shirt. As soon as she saw her friends huddled on the steps and looking under the Taylors' house, she knew they were watching the stranger next door. Trying to step around them, Lucy stumbled, startling Eve, who let out a little cry of surprise. The boy next door immediately turned around and saw them watching him, but his response was a friendly smile and a wave of his hand. His chest was muscular and smooth and what little hair he had was around his navel, going down farther still. They waved back and pretended they were just walking down the steps to the car. Diana was certain he made eye contact with Lucy before turning around and going back to work.

The girls piled into Lucy's silver Mercedes, while Lucy grabbed a small plastic cooler from under the house and put it in the trunk. Once they were on their way down the road to the pavilion, Lucy's hand fidgeted with the dial on her radio. After wading through a marsh creek of white noise and signal pops, she found the sweet spot of one of the Charleston radio stations. The song "Hold On" by Wilson Phillips was playing and she turned up the volume.

One by one the girls began singing with the radio. The song had become an anthem for them, and validation for them as young women. It was empowering and one of those songs that felt good to sing.

Following the beach road as the morning sun was rising from the Atlantic horizon, Diana watched all the houses go by, their shadows bouncing along the road between golden streaks of sunlight. They all looked similar. Mostly simple frame houses on stilts, like giant tree houses in pastel shades, and all of them had beach house names like "Sand Dollar," "Sea Foam," "Beach Comber," "Ocean View," and "Tide Break."

"There's the pier over there," Lucy said.

Diana had never seen an ocean pier. It was a fantastic wooden structure of posts planted in the beach sand, washed over by the waves and sea. The posts rose to tree-limb-like structures that supported the long deck out to a diamond-shaped area at the pier's end. In the center of the diamond sat a small structure that was a Southern interpretation of a Japanese pagoda.

Lucy parked her car on the dirt lot, facing a sand dune covered with sweet grass and sea oats. Donning their sunglasses, they made their way to the boardwalk and up a long ramp to shops selling beach clothing, souvenirs, suntan lotion, and fishing gear. Lucy passed by one of the clothing shops, named Suzy Sunfish, and a large brown-haired woman in a pink muumuu came bounding out of the store.

"Why, there's my little Lucy!" The woman gave her a broad warm hug. Her friendly face and large arms were dark brown from years of island living. She looked very comfortable with herself. A bundle of soft brown hair pulled back in a ponytail made her round face look bigger, and her amber-colored eyes had an honest look of bliss.

"Miss Myrna!" Lucy hugged her in return.

"Child, you staying down at the house for a while, or just in for the day?"

"I'm here for the summer with my friends. You already know Eve."

"How you doing, Evie. My, you've grown tall, but you still thin as a beanpole."

"Hey, Miss Myrna," Eve said.

"And this is Diana Villiers and Maggie Bloomer."

"Good to meet you girls," Myrna said. "Lucy, I'm gonna guess your parents aren't down with y'all." When she gave a nod of her head while cutting her eyes at Lucy, they expected her to say, "I know what y'all are up to." But she said not a word and gave them a big toothy grin of approval. "Y'all better be good now. This place is crawling with a mess of handsome-looking young men." Myrna bellowed with laughter. "Come on in the shop. Just got in some Hawaiian wrap skirts, y'all gonna love 'em!"

The girls followed Lucy into Myrna's store and spent a long time looking at the cute clothes, taking turns trying on the skirts. Lucy bought a skirt and said her good-bye to Myrna, who made the girls promise to keep an eye on her "little Lucy."

From one store to the next they shopped, until they were on the backside looking down the long pier. They stopped for ice cream at the candy shop overlooking the backside. They all ordered ice cream cones, except Eve. She ordered a cup of water and two slices of lemon. With ice cream in hand, the four girls strolled down the pier teeming with fisherman casting their lines off the side, and the tourists watching them. Occasionally they would pass by a small troop of college boys. There would be the occasional "Hey baby!" or hoot from one of them. The behavior of the boys of summer was strange to them. They laughed at how much of a show the boys put on. The warm sun felt comforting on their shoulders, and the summer sea breeze swept through their hair and across the deck of the pier.

Before leaving the pavilion, they walked to the last store on one side, which faced the road. It was a large building with plate-glass windows. One window was emblazoned with a "ABC" logo, while the second had an immense red dot designating the building as a state-licensed liquor store. Maggie entered the store and the other girls stood in front of the giant red dot. They waited for her and watched the people go by. Standing in front of a store selling something they could not lawfully purchase or consume gave them a sense of excitement and a feeling of decadence.

Through the glass window, Diana watched Maggie approach the counter carrying six bottles of rum. She saw the old man behind the counter ask her for her identification. He examined it and looked straight at Diana, rolling his eyes. She could see his chest heave a weighty sigh. Diana quickly turned around and stood there until Maggie emerged from the store carrying a cardboard box with the bottles wrapped inside. After they made their way to Lucy's car, Maggie stowed the box containing the bottles of rum in the trunk.

With the pavilion behind them, the girls made their way off the island along the long narrow bridge across Folly River until the bridge road merged with the causeway that split the expansive marsh of Oak Island Creek. They passed by new condominiums and followed the bridge over Legare Creek and the gray mud of the estuary that was quickly being flooded by the rising tide. A few more miles down Folly Road and they saw the red-and-white sign that read "Folly Shopping Center." It was no more than a dull-looking metal-sided strip mall with a few shops anchored by a Piggly Wiggly grocery store. Porgy's Porch was located down the side street that ran along the shopping center, and Lucy turned down this road to enter the parking lot, rolling to a stop in front of the grocery store.

"I'm going to drop you-all off here. Eve darling, I need a gallon of milk, pint of heavy cream, loaf of bread, package of bacon, eggs, and you might want to get some potato chips or nuts or something."

"Okay, got it," Eve said.

Lucy left the girls to their shopping, turned around in the parking lot, and then made right down the unpaved side street, crawling down the dusty road a few hundred yards to the old seafood market. It was a ramshackle place and for well over a century a number of families had called it home. Because of a boat dock extending into a marsh creek, and its proximity to Folly Road, it had evolved from its early occupants' selling produce from the front porch until it was a well-known landmark selling fresh seafood. The wide front porch had rocking chairs, and above the tin roof of the porch was a weathered sign painted with the words "Porgy's Porch - Seafood & Produce" in white.

An old man in blue denim coveralls and a white T-shirt came out to greet her. He was wearing a John Deere cap that covered his white cotton-like hair. The deep dark lines on his face told the story of a hardscrabble life. He had spent years as a young man working in the fields picking tomatoes and melons, later working on a shrimp trawler. Now he worked the store and his sons and grandsons worked the fields, fished, and harvested crabs and oysters.

She waved at him, grabbed her cooler out of the car, and walked up to meet him in front of the old wooden steps. She gave him a small hug and the two went into the store.

Lucy and the old man emerged from Porgy's Porch about fifteen minutes later. She was carrying her cooler and the old man was carrying an old Budweiser box filled with fruits and vegetables. She opened the trunk and put the cooler in and the old man placed the box of produce between the cooler and the box of rum. Pausing for a moment, he pulled one of bottles of rum out of the box and looked at Lucy, nodding his head in a knowing way. He smiled at her with a chuckle and put the bottle safely back into the box. Lucy tipped the old man and went back to pick up her friends.

Maggie, Diana, and Eve were standing in front of the Piggly Wiggly with bags in hand when Lucy pulled up in front of the shopping center. The three of them were grinning with excitement and bubbling with something they just had to tell Lucy, much like little kids who have had too much sugar and cannot contain themselves.

"Oh my God! You'll never guess!" Diana said.

"What, darling?"

"The boys next door were in there buying beer. They invited us to a party at their house tonight. Said they'd be grilling burgers and have plenty of beer, and there would be a lot of people, some driving down from town."

"Well, it's about time," Lucy said. "I've been wondering when they were going to invite us over. This is going to be fun, girls."

"I'm ready to let my hair down," Maggie said.

"And maybe a little more," Diana added.

Maggie laughed.

"Diana, you are so bad," Eve said.

Diana and Maggie were both grinning, and even cautious Eve seemed genuinely excited. It was a beautiful drive back to the beach house. The sea breeze picked up and blanketed the island.

When they were back at the beach house, the girls were waiting with eagerness to go to the party and meet the boys. The few college parties they had attended had mostly been subdued affairs, since they involved cadets from the Citadel and their fellow College of Charleston students. Both schools were decidedly not party schools. But this time, unlike with parties in town, there would be no parents, housemothers, or senior officers. There was a sense of freedom because they could drink, smoke, and stay up as late as they pleased. It was a soft youthful rebellion without any clash with parents and family.

By six o'clock in the evening, the first cars began to arrive, and though the time of the invitation was six thirty, Lucy suggested that a woman should never arrive at a party too early or on time, since it makes her look overeager. She insisted on walking over after seven o'clock.

Except for Eve, the girls were dressed more provocatively than the casual way they dressed around the house. Maggie had donned a short pink plaid English punk–inspired miniskirt with a tight black knit top and white Keds tennis shoes that she had dyed pink. This was in contrast to Diana's very short blue jean skirt, cream-colored halter top, and flip-flops.

Wrapped tight around Lucy's voluptuous figure was a Lilly Pulitzer print skirt of small green and pink pansies. Her matching lime-green top revealed more curves, with a plunging neckline and ruffled collar. She had completed her beach-dressed-up look with a pair of straw sandals with lime-green trim and straps. In contrast, Eve looked smart in tailored white clamdiggers and a loose-fitting salmon-colored linen blouse, buttoned to the top for the sake of modesty. Curiously, her salmon-colored espadrilles had a heel that made her even taller, giving her a gangly look when she walked. As if one of the tall palmetto trees had uprooted itself and gone for a walk in the wind.

At seven ten the four friends walked next door. The tree lined street, normally devoid of cars, now looked like a parking lot around the house next door. They could hear the sound of M.C. Hammer's "U Can't Touch This" from some stereo inside that caused the whole structure to reverberate like a giant wooden speaker.

"Oh no," Maggie said. "These guys have zero taste in music. If they keep it up, they aren't going to be able to touch this." She pointed to herself and waved her hand from her face down to her body. Diana and Lucy laughed and so did Eve.

For the rest of the night, the music was more of the same. It was top forty radio music: Vanilla Ice, Janet Jackson, Madonna, and more M.C. Hammer.

It was a good crowd, and at its peak there were more than two dozen people milling around, separated into small groups and spilling out of the house and onto the back deck. Some of the crowd they recognized from the College of Charleston, and a good portion were obviously cadets because of their knob-head haircuts. The rest were mostly from Columbia and a few were from out of state and just happened to be staying at Folly for vacation.

The cadets had eaten what few burgers they'd grilled when the party started, but no one seemed to care since the main course was alcohol. The beer flowed freely and here and there a few bottles of whiskey made the rounds. As was to be expected, many of the partygoers drank themselves into a stupor.

The four girls tried their best to keep up with the boys in their consumption of beer. Even so, Diana was surprised at Lucy's abilities as a social drinker. She watched her down a half dozen beers with shots of Jim Beam in between, all before eleven o'clock, yet she still managed to stay as composed and as genteel as she'd always been. Even Eve drank some beer, though Diana was certain she nursed the same can throughout the whole night.

By eleven Diana was feeling very good. The beer and the college boys intoxicated her. Their heavy application of cologne added to her drunken feeling and aroused her sensual side. The current conversation was about something to do with a baseball game, but she lost focus when she realized it had been a long time since she'd last seen Maggie. Scanning the crowd for her bright red hair, she saw Lucy and Eve surrounded by a group of cadets.. It was a burst of laughter from Maggie that told Diana she was on the back deck. She saw Maggie's smiling face behind the sliding screen door: she was standing outside, against the railing of a darkened wooden deck. Beside her were two cadets, both of them young and handsome, and they were laughing about a story involving Colonel Dick and a knob and a haircut. Both of the boys were wearing cargo shorts; one of them was wearing a Citadel T-shirt and the other a white T-shirt under an unbuttoned pale-blue oxford.

Maggie saw Diana and waved for her to come out to the back. Since she was not interested in baseball, she walked out back and Maggie introduced the two young men to Diana.

"This is Andrew, and this is Teddy, right?" The cadet nodded and gave Diana a drunken smile. "And this is my friend Diana," Maggie said.

Andrew shook Diana's hand.

"Pleased to meet you," he said.

When Diana reached out to shake Teddy's hand, he stopped and looked her in the eyes. "Maggie said you were from Nashville." Teddy leaned forward and kissed her on the hand. "That's how we do it in Charleston," he said.

"The boys drove down to stay for the week," Maggie said. "I was thinking we should take a walk down to the beach."

The four grabbed their beers and, under a darkened sky, walked down a narrow path lined with sea oats. On the other side of the dune, the beach glowed with the white of breaking waves while specks of phosphorescence sparkled in the spindrift. This beautiful effervescence made them pause for a moment, and then Maggie grabbed Diana's hand, and the two of them ran down to the edge of the water. Teddy and Andrew followed and both boys let out some kind of cheer.

Moving backward and forward with the rhythm of the waves, they dared the roll of the ocean to come closer. Every time the water got close, the girls would let out tiny shrieks and the boys would laugh at them. Andrew was beside Maggie and Teddy next to Diana, both couples holding hands and making small talk.

Andrew whispered something in Maggie's ear and she nodded her head in agreement.

"Come on," she said, "let's go to our house."

They went up the beach and took the path back to Lucy's house, and the four of them sat down on the steps of the old deck. Diana next to Teddy and Maggie sat next to Andrew. It was dark and the dune blocked any view from the beach.

Teddy produced a thickly rolled joint and a lighter from his side pocket. He lit the white tip and took a deep drag before passing it to Diana, and the joint went around, followed by a second one. Diana was incredibly stoned, as were her companions. Teddy's strong body pressed up against hers and he put his arm around her and squeezed her shoulder. She looked over at Maggie, who was kissing Andrew until she caught Diana's eye and gave her a knowing smile.

"I need to go to the restroom," Maggie said.

"Andrew, will you walk me in?"

He said yes and Maggie and Andrew slipped through the door of the house.

Teddy slowly caressed Diana's shoulder while telling her about growing up in Charleston, but she lost focus about what he was saying because she was focused on him only physically. He was strong and muscular, and she watched his Adam's apple move up and down when he spoke. His right arm was still on her shoulder and he moved closer to her, placing his left hand just above her knee. It felt like a tease, because she wanted him to move his left hand closer to the inside of her thigh. Diana wanted him to move faster.

He leaned forward and kissed her. She kissed him back and they were soon making out, kissing passionately. He pulled her closer, and she moved in closer to him. Diana was soon sitting on his lap, face-to-face, with her legs wrapped around him. She could feel his excitement grow strong beneath her, his hands were now under her halter top, and the feeling of having her breast caressed, even by this cadet's awkward movements, excited her.

She slid off his lap and stood over him, removing her underwear. Her hands grabbed him between his legs and he leaned back and moaned. Diana unzipped his shorts and pulled them down to his knees. He tried to pull her close to him, back on his lap, but she pulled back to get herself in a good spot. When she was ready, she moved forward with her hips raised above his. Diana could feel his clumsy hand moving under her, trying to find the right spot, and once he did, he slid inside her. She felt her body give in to him and she lowered herself onto his lap.

At first he tried to move too fast, but she slowed him down and took control of the movement with a slow grind. It was not long before he popped and she could feel it inside her: that sensation, that immediate sense of warm wetness pushed her over the edge. She let go and felt her body tightly clench up, followed by multiple spasms, and immediately the rush of endorphins numbed her head.

It was one thirty in the morning when Maggie and Diana returned to the cadets' house. Eve was sitting on a brown corduroy sofa talking with one of their neighbors. The young man looked as if he was passed out or asleep, but Eve kept on talking. Lucy was standing with three of the boys in the kitchen, leaning against a counter. She looked as composed and as fresh as she had six hours ago and commanded their attention. They were like puppies at their master's feet at dinnertime, hoping to get a little taste of a meal never meant for them.

Without losing the rhythm of her conversation with the three cadets, Lucy looked at Diana and grinned. Her eyes said, "I know what you've been doing." Diana had seen that same look in her mother's eyes, but coming from Lucy, it felt more like a look of approval.

Maggie and Diana joined the conversation with Lucy and the three young men. One of them was talking about the fall of the Berlin Wall and the end of the Cold War. He voiced his apprehension about what it meant for a career in the military. Because the party had been a success with much alcohol consumed, his speech was more of a ramble than a serious political discourse. The girls soon said their good-byes and walked back to their house.

WALTZING in VIENNA

~7~

SUMMER'S END

Over the next few weeks, the Saturday-night parties at the cadets' house became a regular thing. More often than not, Diana and Maggie would trail off with different college boys, get high, and go make out, or more. Sometimes the girls and the boys next door would go to the boardwalk, walk the pier, and pick up rum, beer, and cigarettes. It was a blithe existence, without a reference point, without boundaries, and their days seemed as if they would never end. For that reason, it was impossible for them to consider that in the near future they would be adults. They had no idea how lucky they were to be so young and free.

Dr. Porter Hayes did return on the Thursday following that first party. Again Eve dressed in her pale-blue shift, but this time she spent an hour doing her hair and makeup, adding color to her otherwise pale complexion. When he arrived he was wearing what appeared to be a new suit, and his hair was neatly trimmed. Porter was a man who cared about his appearance, and while he might have been timorous at times, he was arguably the most handsome professor at the college.

They enjoyed a simple seafood dinner at the Crab Shack and pleasant conversation. Porter had edited Eve's paper, and he reviewed the markup with Eve after dinner. The professor had even brought down one of the college's new portable computers for Eve to use to make the rewrite. Out on loan, the Compaq SLT 386 computer was a beast, weighing in at fourteen pounds. It was at the cutting edge of mobile computing technology with a twenty-megahertz processor, two floppy drives, and a eighty-megabyte hard drive. The loan of the computer and having her paper published gave Eve a sense of confidence and a taste of academia. It was to define her career.

She finished her edits on the following Tuesday, and when Porter returned to pick up the computer, he treated her to dinner at Loggerhead's Beach Grill. By the luck of the draw, the hostess seated them at the best table in the restaurant, a small table isolated in a bay window that overlooked the marsh. As they sat down, the restaurant's radio lost its signal from the top forty station in Charleston, as always, and the manager adjusted the signal to the educational station. When the static cleared, Pachelbel's Canon drifted out from the speakers. As they enjoyed broiled flounder with a glass of Zinfandel, the setting sun streaked the sky with golden bands of clouds. It was romantic without Porter's intending it to be so and it caused Eve to feel less like a college girl and more like a woman.

Eve had felt an immediate intellectual connection with Porter. He was gorgeous, neat, and well-mannered. There was softness to him, and while she often felt ill at ease around boys her age, she could talk openly with Porter. She loved to listen to him speak about art and literature, and when he spoke, it was in the language of the old South. It was with a drawl that was uniquely Charlestonian. He addressed her as Ms. Greene and she addressed him as Dr. Hayes.

Periodically Porter would drive down to see Eve, with the pretense of updating her on the status of her paper. He could have called and told her on the telephone, but he insisted on telling her in person. They occasionally went out to eat, or sometimes it was a visit on the back deck. It was obvious to the other girls that Eve's crush was blossoming into romance.

Throughout the entire summer, the girls would see the stranger next door out on his back porch smoking cigarettes. They would sometimes see him below the house, working on his motorcycle. If ever Diana and Maggie caught Lucy watching him they would try to convince her to go over and introduce herself. She would, of course, give them demure replies, saying that she was not interested, yet she was always the first to notice when he was outside.

By the end of July, their summer together was almost over. It was the Sunday after their last party at the cadets' and they were relaxing in the cool of the house. It was hot outside. A scorching ninety-six degrees and it was only one o'clock. Diana and Maggie were feeling the effects of the beer they had consumed the previous night and they were "mending" on the big leather sofa in the back of the house. Lucy was in her pajamas with a cup of coffee, reading Wharton's *Age of Innocence*, while Eve was reading psychology journals Porter had dropped off on his last trip down to see her.

There was a knock on the door. A firm solid knock, and different from when Porter came to call. Different from when one of the cadets dropped by to say hello, or invite them to go down to the pavilion. When Lucy went to the door and looked through the peephole, she was visibly uneasy. Diana had never seen her so nervous. Lucy was always composed and self-assured. She tried to straighten her hair; this caught Diana's attention, and she and Maggie stopped their conversation to watch Lucy, and find out who was behind the door.

When the door swung open, tall and strong stood the stranger next door. He was wearing black jeans, big leather boots, and a black T-shirt. In his hand he clutched a dog-eared paperback. Lucy froze. She was smiling, quietly looking at him, and hiding behind a strange aloofness.

"Good afternoon," he said. "I'm looking for Miss..." He paused and opened his paperback, pulling out a piece of paper with a name written on it. "Miss Lucy Bonneau."

Though surprised, she tried to remain calm and casually said, "I am Lucy Bonneau."

"Miss Bonneau, the Taylors asked me to leave their house key with you. They asked if you could please pass it along to your mother."

He handed over the shiny key.

"Oh, yes, of course, and what's your name?"

"Harrison," he said. "Harrison Smith."

Lucy looked down. She was staring at the book he was holding. It was a copy of Dashiell Hammett's

Maltese Falcon.

He saw her looking at the book, held it up, and said, "Hammett's masterpiece. *Red Harvest* and *The Dain Curse* were brilliant as well, but Sam Spade has both the intellect and the brawn, a thinking man's detective. Hammett has so much texture and atmosphere. It's heady and gritty."

Lucy's eyes lit up and her body language was much looser and less guarded than when she'd first opened the door.

"I've never read any of his other works. You must be quite the fan."

"Well, yes, I am. I'm partial to writers from that era and I try to read everything. Faulkner, Hemingway, Fitzgerald, Miller, the 'lost generation' as they called them. Such an interesting period in history. I once read the ship's manifest of the *Titanic* to get a sense of time and place. Such a famous disaster that most people consider it the loss of a ship, rather than the loss of fifteen hundred individuals. I wanted to humanize it, and get to know the stories."

"That's very interesting," Lucy said.

"I read just about anything. My creative writing professor always tells me, 'In order to be a good writer, one must be a good reader.' It's the reason I came out to the beach. I wanted to get away from everything and have no distractions. No family, school, or work, just me and my bag of books."

Lucy had a dumb smile on her face, and did not know quite what to say to him. Her silence puzzled him and he smiled back.

"Okay," he said. "I need to get going. Dinner with my folks tonight. You know how that is."

Harrison smiled at Lucy and said good-bye. After

she closed the door, she went over to the kitchen window and carefully opened the curtain. She stood there, dumbstruck, quiet, and with wide-open eyes.

She watched him crank up his motorcycle and pull out of the driveway and onto the road. The deafening roar that had once been so loud it woke her from bed now faded as he rode down the long line of asphalt pavement. The silhouette of him on his motorcycle grew smaller and smaller, and soon he disappeared on the line of a hazy horizon.

When she returned to her spot on the sofa and pretended to read her book, no one said a word. In fact, no one spoke of it during the next day while the girls packed up their belongings and prepared to return home.

For their last meal on the big deck, Lucy fried fresh shrimp that they ate with locally grown corn. It was a good simple meal. The salt-and-pepper shrimp contrasted nicely with the sweet corn. While a freshening ocean breeze helped cool down the day's heat, the thought of going home the next day was sobering. Lucy and Eve cut the evening short, since they wanted to look rested when they saw their parents. However, Diana and Maggie were not quite ready to call it a night, and decided to share one last joint under the starry sky.

"Are you ready to leave and go home tomorrow?" Maggie asked.

Diana laughed at the ridiculousness of the question. Not because of what Lucy and Eve might have wanted, because they were ready to go back to their un-fractured families and beautiful lives. She also knew that Maggie, who had a certain amount of wanderlust, wanted to go somewhere else. Diana was not particularly ready to go home and face her parents in the middle of their divorce. She would have been happiest if she could have stayed at this house by the sea. Waking up every morning to drink her coffee and watch the sun come up.

There was peace here, a quiet calm bathed in ocean breezes, with the time kept by the waxing and waning tide. It all had to end and Diana knew this, so for tonight she pretended that it was her house, and after a second joint she and Maggie lay on the deck and looked up at the stars until they both felt sleepy and decided to go to bed, far earlier than most other nights they had spent there.

Like a coming storm during a sunny day, the reality of family life and the coming fall semester crept back into the girls' consciousnesses. There were tearful good-byes when they loaded their bags into their cars and locked up the beach house. They left together, their cars following one another until they reached Charleston, and then going their separate ways.

By most standards a two-month holiday, especially without parents, is a very long vacation. For the girls, however, the eight weeks were over in what seemed like an instant. It's an ironic contradiction that as people grow older, vacation days and holidays are savored by the drop, but youth squanders those precious moments. Diana and Maggie had enjoyed their carefree days with wanton passion, and while Lucy had enjoyed her summer break as much as the others had, she did feel a little regret for not relishing each day more than the one before it.

Lucy went back to the home she had always known. She went back to the family life that, at least on the surface, was perfect. Money was never an issue, and she spent time with her mother preparing for school, visiting relatives, and readying herself for the new season.

Lucy's social calendar was filled with balls, formal parties, and spending time with her mother attending events at the church and the Lyric Opera Society. Prodded by her mother, she became more involved with the Garden Club and Junior League. The only thing she did for herself was to volunteer at the local library reading storybooks to children on Saturday and Sunday afternoons.

It was different for Eve. While her family's history was just as strongly rooted in Charleston society as Lucy's, her parents saw the Charleston social scene as unnecessary for bringing up their daughter. Eve had joined the same sorority as Lucy, of course, and occasionally attended a Junior League event, but her life was a lot less tangled than Lucy's was. Where her life changed was in her direction in school after her paper was published to minor acclaim. It pushed her to further her academic studies, and she became a favorite of the psychology department and an assistant to Dr. Scott.

At the same time, her relationship with Professor Porter Hayes advanced into a real romance. Despite the twenty years between them, almost a generation, they quickly discovered how well their personalities meshed. They both adored films by Truffaut and Hitchcock, and both appreciated the music of Scarlatti, Bach, and Italian opera. Their tastes in literature and philosophy were more diverse. Porter shared his love for the Victorian playwrights George Bernard Shaw and Oscar Wilde, while Eve piqued his curiosity with the writings of Schopenhauer and Nietzsche. While the timbre of the writings of Nietzsche and Wilde were profoundly dissimilar, like Porter and Eve, the writers' fondness for metaphors and irony supported the counterpoint of their own conversations. Their romance was like a stanza from Bach's "Well-Tempered Clavier." It was a point-against-point perfect fit, and a formula for romantic success. Besides the age difference, there was also the issue of discretion. Porter and Eve worked very hard to keep their relationship a secret to the college faculty, her fellow students and to her parents. At times and in public, Porter was cold to her, to the point where she would question his affections, only to be reassured in private of their intellectual and caring relationship.

For Diana and Maggie, who were attending college on financial aid and working part-time jobs, there were no social obligations or big families to appease. There was little financial help from their families and they had little interest in joining a sorority or social club. Both girls lived on campus and a few weeks remained before they could return to their college dormitories. They were in a holding pattern and stuck in a state of limbo. The summer was not over and they were not ready to assume the life of mundane college coeds.

Putting off the inevitable of finding a job waiting tables or working retail, Maggie had suggested that

Diana stay with her and her mother in Mount Pleasant, but Diana's mother had asked her to come home for the interim. She balked at the idea and relented only after pressing her mother to let Maggie come along with her. Maggie, of course, was ecstatic at the idea, since she had always wanted to visit Nashville, the epicenter of country music, walk down Music Row and go to the Grand Ole Opry.

Maggie and Diana drove out to Nashville in Maggie's pink Karmann Ghia. The nine-hour drive ended as the sun was setting over Diana's mother's house. An older, block-long white Cadillac sat out front in the circular driveway. Maggie immediately fell in love with the house and told Diana she thought it was kitschy. It was a white mini-mansion, a tiny tribute to Scarlett O'Hara's Tara. Thin Romanesque columns in the Southern style sprouted up from a low front porch, supporting a second-floor roof, while white faux chimneys bookended the house. It was more "country tacky" than kitschy. It was as if the house and the car were requirements for those working in the country music business and living in an Elvis-inspired world.

Diana's father had been a recording engineer before his health failed him, mostly from his drinking too much. Her parents' life read like a country music song, complete with honky-tonking, drinking, cheating, and a very public divorce that had ended with her mother's new boyfriend moving into the mini-mansion. His name was Ricky Ray Tyler, he was as young as her father's new girlfriend, and he was an aspiring musician her mother believed would be the next big country music star. Diana's mother was coaching Ricky Ray, paying for his new teeth and

Botox, and helping him meet the right people. She was right too, he would become the next big thing, and more importantly, her mother would become the next big star-maker. She would later earn a small fortune and trade in the mini-mansion for a real mansion on Old Hickory Lake.

Diana and Maggie shared her old room. It was a time capsule of Diana's youth revealing that she was raised as a girlie-girl. The room was dominated by a double bed with a white canopy that sat on cotton candy colored shag carpet. On the opposite side of the room sat a white matching vanity with pictures of Rob Lowe, John Schneider, and Tom Cruise ripped from magazines and taped to the large mirror. There was a ballet dancer topped jewelry box on the vanity and a pink birthday card that read, "Daddy's Princess" leaning against the mirror. The window had a lacy white curtain trimmed in pink. Though dated and tacky, Maggie approved of the "Candy land" bedroom.

For the first time since her parent's separation, indeed, for the first time since she was a little girl, Diana and her mother got along amazingly well. Her mother seemed genuinely happy and Diana thought that perhaps her mother and father were never meant to be, and the divorce was a terrible means to a happy end.

The two girls stayed up late with her mother watching Ricky Ray jam with his band and perfect his vocal skills. They had cleared out the den and set up a performance space. Being this up close and intimate with professional musicians, Diana paid close attention to the band and their instruments. A few of them were session musicians, hired by Diana's mother to give Ricky Ray some much-needed polish. Ricky Ray's guitarist had just finished studio work for Garth Brooks and the Judds, and Diana was fascinated with his finger style guitar picking. He was a large and squat older man, in his sixties and everyone called him Junior. Sometimes he would stand, but most of the time he would sit on a stool looking like a mountain holding a Telecaster guitar.

Back in the day, he had spent time on the road with Merle Haggard, who he called "Hag", Waylon Jennings, George Jones and other Nashville legends. Junior was friends with her father and had spent countless hours in the recording studio with him at the controls. At the end of the night, Junior would teach Diana a few guitar licks and recount stories of great performances with country music legends, both in the studio and on the road. He would also spin tales of wild parties, barroom fights and drunken episodes with Hag and Waylon. These stories of country music gossip and scandal delighted Diana and Maggie.

It was the story that Junior told Diana on the Saturday after they arrived that changed everything. It was nearly one in the morning and the band had finished rehearsing, not because they were tired, but because they were all too drunk. Diana's mother and Ricky Ray had already gone to bed and Junior was sitting on his stool showing Diana how to play "Crazy." He told her that even though Patsy Cline made the song famous, Willie Nelson had written it when he was a struggling songwriter. He talked a lot about Willie and how he had worked with him a couple of years ago when he recorded "Nothing I can Do About It Now" with Diana's Father in the recording booth. Junior told her about the morning he came in to the studio to practice and saw Ricky Ray and Diana's mother having sex in the recording booth. Diana was shocked and Maggie stared off in an uncomfortable silence.

Diana had always thought it was her father's fault. The night her boyfriend brought her back from senior prom, she walked in to find her parents in the middle of an angry fight. Her mother had accused him of having an affair and kicked him out of the house. He tried to return and explain, but her mother called the police who escorted him away.

Junior was unaware Diana did not know the real story. He told her it was her mother's affair with Ricky Ray that ended the marriage, not the other way around. Her father had no clue then and still does not know exactly what caused their marriage to fall apart.

Diana was furious at her mother. It shook her belief in marriage and she wondered why people even bother to enter into a relationship when they are going to eventually cheat and lie. She stayed up all night, crying with Maggie by her side.

As a child she had thought her parents' marriage was perfect, but as a young woman, she saw her mother in a different light. She was disheartened at how her mother had demonized her father and raked him over the coals in divorce court. After a furious and vocal argument with her mother the next morning, she and Maggie piled their bags into the car and took off in a dusty gust of disappointment.

Before leaving town, she and Maggie drove out to the apartment complex where her father was living. She wanted to tell him what she had learned, but she was surprised to find he had known all along but had not wanted to embarrass her mother. His decision to take all the blame came from some kind of respect he held for her mother that Diana could not understand. The lines on his face told her how sorry he was for what had happened, sorry for the life he had led. Before she left he gave her an old cardboard box labeled "Rare Recordings." It was filled with a couple of dozen cassette tapes and an envelope with Diana's name on it. Inside the envelope was a little over a thousand dollars. He told her it was to help with college and was all he could spare. Within a few years, her father's path would go in the opposite direction of her mother's, and he would die a broken man.

The first thing Diana did with the money was to go to one of the downtown pawnshops and buy an old Gibson acoustic guitar. She and Maggie left Nashville and used the rest of the money to take their time on the road before returning to Charleston. They were in no hurry to return, so they meandered, with stops in Memphis to visit Graceland and Beale Street, then off to Clarksdale, Mississippi, for stops at Robert Johnson's crossroads and Red's Juke Joint. They ended their road trip with a drunken week in New Orleans that included seeing some of the best local blues and jazz bands the Big Easy had to offer.

Along the way Maggie taught Diana all she knew about playing guitar, and they listened to the cassette tapes Diana's father had given her. Most of them contained old Hank Williams songs her dad had culled from studio outtakes and forgotten radio show recordings. To make their money stretch they stayed at cheap hotels, staying up late performing the songs from the tapes. They played vamped-up versions of

Williams's "Hey Good Lookin'," "Crazy Heart," and "Lost Highway." Most nights they found themselves at a different bar, occasionally jamming with the house band, and during the day they would find a park or street corner and play for tips. It started as a lark, since Diana knew only a couple of songs, but they were surprised at how much they could make in a few hours. Most of the time people will toss a little money into a hat, but they will pitch in more if the street musicians are two pretty girls. Diana quickly realized this simple fact and would use it later in her music career.

Along with picking up the occasional musician for a one-night stand, Diana and Maggie picked up songs. It was a crash course in rock, blues, and country standards, and by the time they arrived in Charleston the weekend before school started, Diana and her guitar were inseparable. She had learned all that Maggie could teach her, mastering rhythm guitar, and plucking out blues and rock riffs. Diana was a natural musician. It was a gift that her parents had either overlooked or blocked her from developing, even though they worked and lived in the heartland of country music. She was completely at ease belting out cover tunes and classic bar-song.

After they received their dorm assignments, they learned they were no longer suite-mates, and it was a huge disappointment, especially for Diana, since she felt that Maggie was her equal in preferences, desires, and view of the world. Neither before nor after did Diana ever meet another woman with whom she felt such an affinity, such an equal friendship or such a trusting bond. She had always been more comfortable around men, but Maggie was the exception.

It was with a slowly evolving destiny that Diana's dorm assignment paired her with a girl she met only a few times, named Anne-Marie. She was the kind of girl Diana disliked the most, preferring to be called by her full name Anne-Marie instead of Anne, Annie or Marie. There was no southern twang in her voice, instead, there was a chirp that would flutter in pitch with most words, sugar coating her baby talk beyond sweetness. She was a shallow thing who always wore a bright-pink ribbon in her hair, and believed her average figure and mild looks the best on campus. However, it was providence because Anne-Marie's boyfriend lived off campus, so Diana saw her when she first moved in and two other times when Anne-Marie's parents visited her from out of town. With this ghost of a roommate, and since Maggie's assigned roommate was another senior she did not like, Diana had the whole room to herself and Maggie crashed on Anne-Marie's slightly used bed.

Maggie returned to her old job, tending bar at Big Cat's Pub on Broad Street, and managed to get Diana a gig playing acoustic guitar on Wednesday and Thursday nights. For their downtime the two hit the pubs and the bars around Charleston, checking out the latest bands to come to town and chasing after boys, most often the boys in the bands. Maggie's senior year was just as much fun for Diana as it was for her. By being Maggie's wing-woman, Diana developed her own tough-girl sexy panache. Her first two years in college had changed her from a disheartened high school girl to a local groupie and musician. Bold, brash, and not afraid of anyone, she had a femme fatale swagger that was to define her in later years.

The next summer Diana, Lucy, and Eve returned to Folly Beach without Maggie. She had left town soon after graduation with a bachelor's in religious studies and a minor in philosophy. Diana had taken Maggie out to celebrate her graduation and, unexpectedly, Maggie had told her she had joined the Peace Corps and intended to leave for India in one week. It was a bolt from the blue to Diana. She had assumed Maggie would stay in town. They had even talked about sharing an apartment once Maggie had a "real job." For the rest of the night and some weeks thereafter Diana was disheartened that her friend, her first true female friend, had abandoned her, or at least it felt that way to her.

~ 8 ~

MARRIAGE AND MUSIC

Folly Beach was not the same without Maggie, but though Diana had lost a friend she felt was hip and a free spirit, she found a connection with the intellectual feminism of Lucy. It was despite the fact that she and Lucy trod contradictory paths, one a repressed Southern debutante and the other on her way to becoming a rock star and a Southern decadent.

It was the summer before their senior year, and the last time of real substance they would spend together and the last summer they would spend at Folly Beach. It was also the last time they would be in a position where relationships, commitments, and occupations did not consume them. They had made the realization that the future was about to be far more complicated than being an undergraduate attending a small Southern college. Lucy had made plans for her near future, while Diana was simply trying to figure out what to do next. Eve, of course, was nervous about deciding what path to take now that she felt the pull of her relationship with Porter. He had suggested she move in with him, even though they downplayed their relationship with friends and family. In fact, they often absolutely denied one ever existed. As during the summer before this one, he showed up every Thursday and Sunday afternoon, claiming that his visits were school-related.

Porter's visits served as punctuation during the weeks of carefree relaxing by the beach. The girls' nights featured the same ritual as the summer before of waltzing in Vienna after the evening meal. There were countless parties at the house next door, and while Lucy held court and Diana went on the prowl, Eve had no designs on any of the young men. Still, she enjoyed going to the parties to watch all the players navigate the tangled map of college relationships. As a young psychologist, she was more interested in observing relationships than in examining her own personal journey. Because of her aversion to boys her age, she had left open emotional places, places of love, romance, and passion. However, the measured steps Porter made in getting to know her were slowly filling those open spaces. Those carefully measured steps finally overfilled her emotions.

"But what if my parents found out?" Eve asked.

She was on the kitchen telephone wearing her bathrobe. Her hair was still wet from a shower she had cut short when Porter called.

"Well, you know I still don't feel comfortable enough to do that now," Eve said.

The wall-mounted telephone had a long curled cord that led to the handset. It was usually kinked up and tangled; Eve straightened out the cord during her long conversation.

"Don't say that. You know how I feel about you."

She paused before saying anything else as the tears began to roll along her bottom eyelids.

"Fine. Yeah, okay. I'll see you soon. Of course I feel the same way."

Eve placed the handset back into the cradle of the phone, carefully straightened out the cord, and just stood there. Both Lucy and Diana expected her to say something, but she looked at them with a face contorted with conflict and said nothing.

Porter had asked her to stay with him before she returned home from summer break, before her parents expected her back home. While she was not comfortable with the idea of deceiving her parents, Porter had finally convinced her, and she packed her bags as quickly as she could. She drove to Charleston in the midafternoon, leaving Lucy and Diana to spend the rest of the week together. A fuzzy gray mood lifted once Eve drove away, and Lucy and Diana's conversations became more vivid, loud, and passionate.

They enjoyed long talks about literature and music in a marijuana-fueled fog, staying up late, laughing and telling jokes. Occasionally Diana would pull out her guitar and belt out long versions of "Louie, Louie" or "Jumpin' Jack Flash" while imitating the styles of Mick Jagger and Keith Richards. When Saturday crawled in, Diana wanted to forgo the last party of the summer. It was curious to Lucy, because Diana, who was such a party girl, adored the attention from the boys. It was because, she said, she wanted to hang out at the house and relish their last night.

Diana was so different from Lucy in family, friends, and the way she lived her life, but she saw Lucy as the wise older sister she had always wished to have. Her mother had always been aloof and cold, and it was worse now because of her success as a star-maker in Nashville. She had elevated her lifestyle far above the one she'd had when she was married to Diana's father. Diana had always been a daddy's girl, but his drinking and string of girlfriends had caused his lifestyle to crash and burn. Lucy filled the void from her parents' disappearing support.

Diana had developed a strong respect for Lucy, almost an admiration, though she would never, could never be like her, and while Lucy on no account would want to walk in Diana's cowboy boots, she told Diana how much she respected her tenacity and ability to "give way to her desires."

"That's what your problem is," Diana said.

"My problem? And what is that, dear?"

"That you don't give way to your desires."

"My desires?" Lucy said. "While I do not judge the way others live, I do judge the way I live, and I guess I am my mother's child. Perhaps my life will be like hers. I'll marry and have some kids and write in my spare time. There's nothing wrong with that."

"Oh, I don't believe that, Lucy. Do you know what you are? You're a reluctant debutante."

"I know it's not a thing for you, dear, but it's part of my family's traditions and heritage."

"But do you enjoy it?"

"Yes, of course, dear."

"That's a bunch of bull. I think you want a whole lot more than that. You're gonna be the next Flannery O'Connor, writing great books that college kids will read during their freshman year about some dark Southern story."

"And live on a farm raising birds? Not hardly. While I'd love to go to Paris and write novels, I need to think about more practical things."

"That's not you, Lucy. If you don't recognize it you will never be happy."

When they returned to campus for their senior year, life became more complicated and they saw less and less of one another. Throughout the fall semester, they met for coffee a few times, and once Lucy and Eve showed up to see Diana's band perform at an outdoor concert sponsored by the college. Diana had become a serious musician, and her schoolwork suffered from missed classes and hangovers during morning lectures. She had little interest in going to class. Finishing school became a minor priority. After various bands with equally various names and music styles, she had a solid-sounding all-girl band that she had named Crazy Hearts after her favorite Hank Williams song. They'd all clicked and had the same vision of tough rock 'n' roll chick attitude.

They were playing more gigs out of town and practiced regularly in an old warehouse down by the Ashley River. In an endeavor to save money, she and her bandmates moved into the dingy warehouse, setting up folding screens in the back to partition their beds. A slab table served as a kitchen, fitted with a microwave, coffee maker, and small fridge one of the girls had mysteriously provided after she left her apartment on campus. Despite the lack of creature comforts and having to weather the cold unheated space, the band was optimistic, buoyed by a growing number of fans who came in droves to each show. Their legion of thirsty followers delighted bar owners and small venues, keeping them in high demand.

Their rising success was due in part to a live recording of one of their songs making the rounds on college radio stations across the Southeast. A couple of minor record labels had taken notice too, and this interest piqued the curiosity of local newspapers and live-music devotees. Touted as the unsigned next great band, they were rising on a slow swell that lay before the wave of national success they would soon enjoy.

Diana had gone her own way and had lost touch with Lucy and Eve. During the spring semester, their last, the three young women never had time to meet even for coffee. Even Lucy and Eve saw less of one another. It was a busy time for all of them.

Eve became more involved with the psychology department, attending conferences and seminars, and working as a teacher's aide for Dr. Scott. She published a second paper, "Interpersonal Relationships within College Dating Cycles." Whatever free time she had was spent with Porter and she was absent from just about everything else.

Even though everyone on campus knew they were dating, the two maintained their facade of a student-professor relationship. This charade broke down after spring break. Eve had accompanied Porter to Dublin for a tour of Trinity College and an opportunity for him to search through the school library's collections of Wilde, Yeats, and Joyce. It was pure joy for Porter and the experience inspired him in his own academic pursuits during the years to come.

The ancient Trinity Library is a cathedral of literature, made magnificent by its great domed ceiling and charming by its massive collection of leather-bound books. Eve had never seen Porter so spirited and happy, even giddy.

They spent three days there and on the last day of his research, a Wednesday, she watched a string quartet assemble in the hall of the library. Porter was beaming, and when the musicians launched into Beethoven's Razumovsky No. 8 in E Minor, his favorite quartet, she knew something was up. A small crowd watched as Porter got on one knee and proposed to her. She said yes and he cried with joy. There was something dramatically romantic in the proposal, and for most young girls the moment would have been magical, but for Eve there also was a sense of satisfaction and security in both her future as a professional, and the man to whom she would be married.

The freshly engaged couple took a stroll down Nassau Street past College Park and crossed over to Clare Street, and walked down a long line of dim row houses until they reached Merrion Square Park. It was a beautiful spring day and the grass was greener than any grass they had ever seen. Along the way Porter stopped to pose with a reclining statue of Oscar Wilde, and as evening encroached into the park, the skies gave the green lawns a pinkish glow.

As the sun sank low to the city's horizon, the two hopped into a taxi and asked the driver to take them to a good pub near the Abbey Theatre. They asked for one with a bit of history and character and the driver obliged by taking them to the Flowing Tide, directly across the street from the theater. Its stone-and-stained-glass facade made them feel like Dubliners, as if they were drinking with Joyce himself. Instead of the ubiquitous pint of Guinness that every tourist must drink, Eve ordered a glass of white wine and Porter settled on a pot of Earl Grey tea.

Revived from the day's excitement, Porter and Eve enjoyed Shakespeare's *Comedy of Errors*, performed at the Abbey with an Irish zeal that pushed the farcical play into the realm of slapstick. It was a fun and beautiful end to a very charming day, and during the next few days the happy couple toured the city with literary gusto. When they returned to Charleston word quickly got out that the two were engaged to be married, and Eve and Porter no longer hid their affection. The student and the professor became the subject of gossip and speculation for the rest of the spring season. Eve's life had sped up to a frenetic pace.

It was also a busy time for Lucy, dividing time between doing what her mother expected of her and occasionally spending time with Aunt Catherine talking about literature. Never in want of a suitor, she was constantly approached by young men asking her out to dances and movies. She did date often, but always kept them at arm's length—that is to say, she gave them nothing more than a good-night kiss.

While her friends had their steadies, earned their

"MRS" degrees, and graduated into marriage, Lucy made a conscious decision to attend graduate school and avoid a serious relationship. Making the choice to continue her education, or rather, not to get married and have children, was the most rebellious thing she had ever done. It surprised many of her father's family. Indeed, the news that she had been accepted into the creative writing program at the University of Virginia arrived while her house was filled with aunts, uncles, and cousins of the Bonneau family.

Bonneaus had owned the house for over 170 years, and her father, the only son of five children, had inherited the grand dame of a home on the Battery. It was a family legacy and often pointed out by the carriage tours that passed by as one of the great homes of antebellum Charleston. It was a monstrously huge house for any family, and there was room aplenty since Lucy was an only child. Accordingly, each year Lucy and her parents hosted a family reunion during the long week before Easter.

The weekend had always ended with a great Sunday dinner after Easter services, prepared by Lucy's mother and aunt Catherine. The family feast included quiches, stews, fresh breads, and vegetables drenched in truffle sauce and other glazes. All of this surrounded the traditional rack of lamb cooked in the French style. It was at the Easter feast during spring break that Lucy's father shared the news of the extension of her academic career with her extended family. Though she knew her father was proud and her mother happy, despite apprehensions about her leaving home, he gave the news with such reserve that it sounded as if it were to be a family secret. A deafening silence followed from an audience who thought it just plain wrong or simply did not care. Aunt Catherine was the first to congratulate her. Of course, she was not a Bonneau. Furthermore, as most of them knew, she had completed the same program at the University of Virginia before returning to Charleston to write poetry and move in with her old college roommate.

Even in modern times, a woman attending graduate school, especially a liberal arts program, is a curiosity in certain circles. Scholarship is usually the domain of the unattractive and nonmarrying type, and Lucy was definitely not in either of these two categories. Beautiful, young, and well-bred, she was at the top of the Charleston social scene and, to her relatives, a real catch. Why she would want to waste the best years of her life was puzzling to them.

Eventually the gray clouds left behind by her Bonneau kinfolk drifted away along with the gossip and speculation put forth by neighbors and friends. When early May rolled around, Lucy was basking in the idea that she was breaking out to become her own woman. She and her family celebrated a very fine graduation during a very fine Charleston afternoon, made beautiful by the College of Charleston's tradition of the graduates' wearing all white.

Outside, under the live oak trees and on the green of the college, hundreds of young ladies dressed in crisp white summer dresses lined up, each of them clutching a single red rose. Young gentlemen, the male graduates at the college, flanked them, and they wore black bow ties and formal white jackets adorned with red rose boutonnieres. To the unknowing, the scene might have looked like some strange mass wedding, but to Charlestonians it was part of a genteel tradition that stretched back to the old days.

Eve had decided not to walk, instead choosing to attend the American Conference on Intrapersonal Psychology in Washington. The prestigious conference trumped the graduation, and since her parents were in a very acerbic mood over her engagement to Porter she saw no reason to go through the ceremony of graduation.

Lucy saw the ceremony as a moment of womanhood and she wanted to make her parents proud of her. She had always been very close to both her mother and her father, and she was walking on air as she accepted her diploma. The weeks that followed saw Lucy busy with preparations and plans for her move to Charlottesville.

May twenty-first began as an ordinary Friday, but quickly became a date Lucy would forever remember. After a shopping trip with her aunt Catherine, she returned home to find a police cruiser in front of her house. Two uniformed officers were standing on her front porch, speaking with Mrs. Wentworth, their next-door neighbor. When they saw Lucy and her aunt, they stopped their conversation, and she could tell by their eyes that something very bad had happened. It was a suspicion confirmed when Mrs. Wentworth began crying and looked at Lucy with a deep pitiful sympathy.

Time is a very strange thing, or at least the perception of it. When there is tragedy, the pauses between conversations hang indefinitely, and Lucy waited for this pause to end so she could hear the thing that would probably tear her down. The moment was made surreal by a sea breeze that shifted to the north and made the rustling sound in the trees seem louder than usual.

"Ms. Lucy Bonneau?" the older officer asked.

"Yes," Lucy said.

"Ms. Bonneau, your parents were involved in an automobile accident," he said. "Your mother is in the trauma ward right now and your father…"

Realizing his delivery sounded like a police report and that this was someone's daughter, he stopped short. Instead of looking at Lucy, he looked directly into her eyes. They were swelling with sadness and in an instant he changed from a police officer to a human being filled with empathy and compassion.

"Your father didn't make it." The officer tried to say something to her but stumbled over his words, and all he could get out was, "I'm sorry."

The words *didn't make it* made her heart sink to her feet. Her purse fell out of her hands and she dropped the shopping bags she was carrying to the same place where her heart lay. Lucy felt her feet become rooted to the ground and her skin felt like the bark of a tree. It was what Daphne must have felt when she tried to avoid capture by Apollo. The same sea breeze ruffled her hair and the noise deafened her. She could not bear to hear another word.

Her aunt asked about the details and the officers explained that a car driven by an intoxicated woman had crossed over the line and collided with the Bonneaus' head on. Lucy's father had died on impact and her mother was still in the trauma unit. When it was time to go to the hospital, Aunt Catherine took Lucy by the hand and uprooted her from where she stood. They drove in silence to see her mother.

During the days that followed, long days with little sleep, Lucy learned that her mother had broken her left femur and cracked multiple ribs. She had survived by a small miracle, and the doctors all agreed she would not walk for months, perhaps ever. Aunt Catherine took care of all the "business" for someone who has passed away, working with her father's four sisters to carry out his last wishes.

The day before Lucy's father was to be buried in a private ceremony, Aunt Catherine and the Bonneau sisters opened the family house to neighbors and friends. Her mother was still in the hospital and by now Lucy's initial shock had worn off. Over the course of the day, no fewer than two hundred people arrived to pay their respects, some of them bringing food, and all of them bringing condolences. Her father had been a respected real estate lawyer and known as a prudent but fair man. Esteemed by his fellow parishioners at the Huguenot Church, he had been an active member in the Huguenot Society.

Lucy had been aware that her father was well known, but the massive outpouring of grief surprised her, and as the day wore on it overwhelmed her. In front of the big window in the living room overlooking the front yard, she stood for a very long time wedged between her aunt Sissy and her grandmother Bonnie Bonneau. She grew tired of the sympathetic looks from people she barely knew and of hearing, "You poor thing" repeatedly. It was just as stifling as it was depressing, and she desperately needed to escape.

Lucy found her way out to the garden. Somehow

she managed to leave the room undetected, relying on her aunts to greet the next round of visitors. Hundreds of flowers perfumed the air and the blaze of red and pink azalea bushes stood in sharp contrast to the heaviness of the house and the monotonous black worn by her family. Standing near a drooping magnolia laden with white waxy blossoms, she watched a hummingbird dart from flower to flower along a twisted vine of honeysuckle. She remembered watching the hummingbirds with her father when she was a little girl. They would sit on the old metal bench near the tree and he would tell her about how the Gullah people believed that hummingbirds were messengers between the worlds of the living and the dead. Time and space had no meaning for them and they vibrated so quickly that they slipped between the seen and the unseen. If only she could vibrate as fast, she might be able to see her father one last time.

"Miss Bonneau," a baritone voice called out.

Lucy turned to find a striking young man wearing a marine uniform. Well built in his dress blues, he had a halo of short blond hair circling under his cap. His skin was swarthy and his eyes were crystal blue.

"You are Ms. Lucy Bonneau, are you not?" he asked.

"Yes."

"Please allow me to introduce myself," he said. "I am Second Lieutenant Theodore Pendleton, United States Marine Corps, Parris Island, at your service."

Such a formal introduction almost made her laugh, almost made her smile for the first time in so many days.

"Lucy Bonneau," she said, "pleased to meet you. But please call me Lucy."

"Yes, ma'am. I wanted to give you my condolences. Your father was a fine man. My father was one of his clients and I had the pleasure of meeting him when they were getting a piece of my father's property rezoned for a hotel."

"Thank you, Lieutenant Pendleton," she said.

"Please call me Theo, ma'am."

"I will if you call me Lucy."

"Yes, ma'am, Lucy," he said. "My father and mother are inside, but I wanted to meet you before I returned to base."

"I appreciate you taking the time to visit."

"You are welcome. May I walk you back to the house?"

"Certainly."

To a casual observer, the two might have looked like an elegant couple on their way to a formal event. Lucy's smart and simple A-line black dress complemented his dark dress uniform jacket. Since Lucy did not feel like talking, as she had been making small talk for most of the day, she asked about his life and about being a marine. It was a lifelong dream for him and he explained that he was not the type to go to a party school. He told her his dedication had paid off in his being accepted into the NROTC unit at the Citadel and completing Officer Candidates School. After graduating with a civil engineering degree, he had recently completed basic training at Parris Island and was now stationed there, working as an engineer in base operations.

The sun had marched down South Battery Street and was hanging low like a beacon over the Ashley River. Lucy and Theo stopped at the bottom of the wide staircase that led up to the front porch. Late-afternoon light, muted by the streetscape, cast long shadows across the yard as a carriage clopped loudly down the street as if to create an interval before they were to say good-bye. The sound of Theo's parents walking out the front door with Aunt Catherine broke that natural moment. Catherine said something quietly to them before they walked down to join Theo. Before returning to the house, Aunt Catherine made eye contact with Lucy and gave her a warm smile.

The Pendletons stopped to tell Lucy what a "fine man" her father had been and that they hoped her mother would have a quick recovery. "It was such a tragedy," they said. "Terrible that such a thing should happen to such a good family." Like so many people she'd met today, they told her that if there was anything they could do, she should feel free to call them. Of course, they were just words.

Theo's mother was a kindly-looking woman, but his father, steeped in old Southern tradition, stood aloof. His navy blazer was just a little too tight and he wore khaki-colored pants and suede saddle oxfords. His red necktie was as crisp as his white dress shirt, and a tan Panama hat was perched on top of his round head. He may have been an older man, but his time at the Citadel as a younger man was still apparent.

When they said good-bye to Lucy, the old man nodded to Theo and told him it was time to go. Theo waited to speak until his parents were several steps away.

"Good-bye, Lucy." He hesitated for a moment, to catch his breath and courage. "May I call on you?"

"Yes. Of course," Lucy said.

His presence in the garden slowed down the hummingbirds. There was familiarity in the way he spoke with his slow Charleston drawl. As archaic as they sounded, Lucy found his words charming. Her father would have approved of this young man and deemed him perfect for her, and his family an ideal match for theirs. There was comfort in this. She thought about that old cliché used in abundance in romance novels, but he really was "an officer and a gentleman." This broad-shouldered marine officer was conventional, respectful, and from a good family whose roots went back to before the Revolution. Such a Southern ideal that she could hardly believe he was real.

The day after Lucy buried her father she made the difficult decision, the right decision, to postpone graduate school, stay home, and take care of her mother. She spent long days and nights at the hospital and watched her mother undergo two long and painful surgeries. One of them involved the insertion of a titanium rod and numerous pins to reset her leg. It was a full month before her mother could return home. This long and trying interval gave Lucy time to turn the living room into a bedroom for her mother, since the master was upstairs. The rented hospital bed was dressed up and Lucy faced it toward the big window, letting sunlight flood the room. Lucy had mixed those hospital things meant to make her mother more comfortable with the antiques and things that were familiar to her. There were family heirlooms and keepsakes.

Her mother's recovery became Lucy's full-time job, but it did give her time to write and read. Even so, the sadness and depression of her mother dampened even the best day to a point where Lucy felt like reading only a few pages or staring at a blank page. It was a long journey of excruciating physical rehab and rounds of antibiotics and pain pills.

Four weeks after her mother's return, when Lucy felt all alone, isolated from the real world like the Lady of Shalott, Second Lieutenant Pendleton did call again. His first visit was made during leave on a Saturday afternoon. It was a warm day in July and Lucy made ham sandwiches, deviled eggs, and iced tea that they enjoyed in the garden. He talked about himself, about what he would do when he left the marine corps after his enlistment ended. His ideal life included going to work for his father, getting married, and having children. Ordinarily a date like this would have been a small thing for Lucy, a date with a nice boy on a nice day that would lead nowhere. However, this date was a release from the drudgery of being a caretaker. It was a blast of youthful spirit, and Theo's talk about the future gave her hope for her own.

Success came slowly for her mother. The first move was from a wheelchair to a walker, and by the end of the year her mother was able to leave the house using a cane. Theo's visits increased and, though he lived on base, he became a constant visitor at Lucy's house, and their dating could be best described as courting. It was good for her mother as well, not only because Theo aided Lucy in getting her mother out of bed, or in and out of the wheelchair, or helping with her physical therapy, but also because her mother's spirits began to rise as she saw their romance blossom. The vivaciousness of youth warms not only the hearts of young men and women, but also those of their parents.

The following February, when her mother could not take the cold weather any longer, Lucy's aunt Catherine suggested they take a vacation to a warmer climate. Even with Theo around, she could see how badly Lucy needed a fresh perspective, and she arranged for two weeks in Hawaii. At first Lucy's mother did not want to go, but after Aunt Catherine tempted her with warm weather, luaus, and endless pineapples and macadamia nuts, her mother agreed.

When they returned, Lucy found Theo on the front steps of their house waiting for them. He was in his dress blues, and after he helped Lucy, her mother, and her aunt with their bags, he took Lucy to the back garden. The last few days of February were not as cold as when they had left for the Pacific, and in the soft evening light, Theo dropped to one knee and proposed to Lucy. He had briefly seen her in Hawaii but still said he could not be without her, could not take her being away for so long, and wanted to marry her and have her with him every day.

Their marriage was in April and was not the grand spectacle of a typical Charleston socialite's wedding, like those of the other young women she knew. It was a relatively simple ceremony with Eve as the matron of honor and three bridesmaids culled from friends at the church. Lucy did not want to turn it into a spectacle; just friends and family and everyone who was important to her was there, except for Diana. She was on tour with her band far away, and their friendship seemed far away too.

Theo's best friend Andrew was his best man, along

with three other fellow marines as groomsmen. Decked out in their formal marine uniforms, they gave an overwhelming air of regimentation to the ceremony. The service held at the old Huguenot Church, her family's church, was the last service Lucy was to attend there. Theo's family was Episcopalian, and for generations they had attended St. Philip's Church. Lucy wanted to support her husband, so she joined the congregation when she became part of the Pendleton family, much to the disappointment of her Bonneau kinfolk.

Also for the support of her husband, she moved to Beaufort, and the happy couple rented a cottage off base. It was just before their first wedding anniversary that she gave birth to twin boys. It was difficult at first. Their two-bedroom cottage seemed small, especially considering that they had both grown up in large Charleston city houses. For another year and a half they struggled on Theo's pay, and Lucy began to miss living in Charleston and seeing her mother. She often took the hour-and-a-half drive to see her mother and aunt Catherine, taking the babies. It all changed when Theo's enlistment was up and he chose not to reenlist.

Immediately they began looking for a rental in Charleston, since they both felt it natural to move back to the city they loved. Theo's father was developing a new hotel in partnership with the Hilton chain and he wanted Theo to take the lead. It was an exciting time, a time for change, and a promising future lay ahead. The young couple was even more delighted, thrilled tremendously, when Lucy's mother gave them the house on the Battery, the Bonneau house, and her mother chose to move out to the old cottage on Folly Beach.

The years that followed were happy and filled with success. Theo's career took off on a meteoric rise based on the success of his first project. The Hilton development division took notice and asked him to leave his father's private development group and come on board with it. His relationship with his father had always been tense, because his father was a hard man to please. At times he was a very coarse man, sometimes brutal with his language and derogatory comments. He had little regard for Theo, or for Theo's sister or mother.

Theo's decision to work for the Hilton group was an easy one and he began as part of the Hilton corporate development team based in Virginia. He soon found himself as an itinerant employee, father, and husband, whose success depended on his traveling two-thirds of the year.

Lucy, Theo, and their sons had to adapt, and that they did, with Lucy raising the children in the grand house on the Battery. Often her mother or aunt Catherine helped during Theo's long stints out of town. After just ten years with the hotel chain, he began working with the European division, traveling to Europe often and making his family very comfortable financially. Theo was at the top of his game.

She watched her boys grow up and spent a lot of time with her mother, though she was unaware that time was short for Mrs. Bonneau. Her mother's passing was very hard for Lucy and since Aunt Catherine had moved away to Portland, she leaned heavily on Eve for support. They began seeing each other regularly.

When Porter passed away, Lucy was there for Eve too. Not that Eve was torn apart as much as Lucy had been when her mother died, but their friendship grew because of it and they recognized that this friendship was the one thing from their past that had been positive for both of them. As women and as mothers who were proud of their sons, they shared their old memories and their kinship.

WALTZING in VIENNA

~9~

LA DOLCE VITA

E ve Hayes was always on time. Even if she
arrived early, she would sit in her car and wait
for the exact time of an appointment, show, or
reservation. Time, like so many of the other less
important things, was one of many uptight habits that
defined her fastidious existence. It was no surprise
that she had arrived at the Footlight Players Theatre
early enough to get a parking space on the street in
front of the theater. Yet she stayed in her car writing
notes for her next radio show as everyone went in. It
was also true that she preferred not to arrive early at
public events, so as to avoid making small talk. Large
crowds made Eve feel awkward and uncomfortable.

As soon as the alarm on her telephone signaled it
was ten till seven, she put away her production notes
and sauntered into the theater. She was wearing a pair
of high-waisted navy gabardine slacks that highlighted
her slender frame. An ivory-colored short-sleeved
cashmere sweater softened her look.

The theater's very old visage looked as if someone
had painted bricks peeking from behind layered

stucco and paint to make it appear weathered and worn. Of course, the theater's ancient brick walls were real, and the fading stucco was the victim of over 150 years of salty sea air and hurricanes that had breached the city's storm walls. The large rounded door frames were evidence that this building had once been a horse stable; the structure was much older than the eighty-year-old theater itself. To the right of the door was a small marquee that read:

Spoleto USA Intermezzi Series Presents
Malcolm Hayes, Performance Artist
Thursday at Seven O'Clock

The crowd in the lobby was sparse, since most of the patrons of this sold-out event were already in their seats. Eve passed off her ticket to the doorman and walked down to her reserved seat in the front row. She took her place, and within five minutes the last few stragglers took their seats and the house lights faded.

The old velvet curtains were cranked open to reveal a young woman in her early twenties holding a microphone. Her brown hair was long and straight, and it rolled like a wave around her head as she turned from side to side. She was wearing a fifties-inspired dusty-pink raw-silk skirt, cut to just above her knees, and a sleeveless ivory-toned silk blouse with a wide collar. Her look had a touch of haute couture and a heavy dose of vintage chic. Behind her were two synthesizers, one above the other on a black metal stand, and a black stool. A microphone on a boom stand hovered above the top keyboard and a laptop computer sat on a small table to the right of the keyboard. On the rear wall of the stage were three massive movie screens in a straight row.

A spotlight came up on the space where the young girl was standing. With a plucky confidence, she smiled and surveyed the packed house. Right away Eve noticed her bright-white teeth when she smiled. She judged people by their teeth, and this young woman had nonveneered perfection. She was impressed.

The young girl raised the microphone to her plump red lips.

"Ladies and gentlemen, my name is Riley Gadsden, special events manager for Spoleto Festival USA. I welcome you to the Footlight Players Theatre for another night of the Spoleto USA Intermezzi series. Tonight I have the great pleasure of introducing performance artist Mr. Malcolm Hayes. He presents for the first time his original symphony of images and sounds, *Voice of a Hurricane*."

She stretched her arm out to the left side of the stage. This signal brought Malcolm from behind the curtain. He looked like his mother in many respects. He was tall and lean, his gait rather gangly, but his shoulder-length hair was dark, almost black. There was something deeply mysterious about Malcolm; it was in his eyes, which were neither blue nor brown. He wore a halo of melancholy. Beneath his black sports coat was a deep-blue dress shirt. He was not as confident on the stage as Riley, but he managed to take his position behind the keyboard stand without incident. Riley's spotlight faded and she exited to the right of the stage, while a pool of deep-blue light emphasized Malcolm's position on the stage.

"Ladies and gentlemen, in all things one can find

music."

Malcolm's voice was a little shaky. He paused for three seconds that to him seemed like three minutes.

"Our planet sings in harmony as it revolves around the sun, and the sun and stars hum along with the rest of the heavens. Over the past year, I have collected hundreds of film clips of hurricanes, and sampled their audio, tuning these sounds across the keyboard. My orchestra is a tempest, my instruments the wind, water, and crash of storms on the land."

Malcolm turned and, with a few keystrokes on his laptop, activated the three projectors mounted overhead. The first images to appear on the screens were of swirling hurricanes, one on each screen. They were satellite images, disembodied from any map, and they danced across the stage, from one screen to the next. It was interplay of weather, a dance of wind. As the images began to appear, Malcolm played the two keyboards, producing harmony from sampled instances of wind. More images appeared on the screen.

There were video clips of rain, oceans, and tides captured in geometric frames that were layered on other images, both moving and static. Malcolm mixed in sounds of water and waves. His images of rain and wind danced to the syncopated rhythm invoked from his keyboard. The interplay of images began to show the effects of storms on boats, beaches, and homes. A swirl of airborne cars and debris danced across the screens like ugly mechanical ballerinas. His music intensified as he included the sounds of creaking wood, and crashing homes and trees. It was a cacophony of sounds, a dense mixture of images and clips that climaxed into a wall of sound before it abruptly ended and faded into the sound of a gentle ocean wave.

The last swath of images showed the aftermath of storms, tranquil debris-filled beaches, images of personal effects floating in the water in a quiet but destructive calm. His music was now subdued, a light and steady sound of an ocean breeze and waves lapping on the shore. It was a contemplation of the quiet after a crisis, when adrenaline no longer flows and exhaustion takes over. It was Malcolm's reflection that the natural world can erase the human things, which mark the earth, easily and without conscience.

When his performance ended after fifty-eight and a half minutes, there was no sound and the three screens faded to black. The only light in the whole theater was the blue light that bathed Malcolm. The final sound was Malcolm quietly saying, "Thank you," to the thunderstruck audience. The same audience immediately launched into a roar of applause. Malcolm, who had never performed in front of such a large audience, was enthralled at the response, and his mother Eve was in tears. She had never seen this side of him, never seen him so forceful, so in command of both the drama of a performance and the emotions of people. It had always been her opinion that Malcolm lived too much in his head to even consider the emotions and feelings of others, much less strive to create something so powerful as this.

Once the house lights were up and the crowd was making its way out of the theater, Eve could hear people talk about her son. She could see how pleased they were with his performance.

Inside the crowded lobby, Malcolm's new fans lined up to meet him. Whether they had enjoyed his performance or not did not matter: they wanted to meet this unknown musical artist, since the overwhelming response to his performance surely indicated he was the next rising star. Eve looked on with satisfaction, like a mother watching her teenager hit a home run or score a touchdown.

Her son, with his myriad conflicted emotions, had found a way to express himself. Malcolm had always been an intelligent child, and so deeply emotional that Eve had become fearful that his integration into mainstream society would be difficult. Ironically, her fears and preemptive parenting were what had pushed him closer to the fringe. Her fears were gone and tonight she was the proud mother, joining in the long line to give him his laurels. As she approached him she saw sheer happiness on his face, a look she had not seen since he was a little boy. Standing next to Malcolm was the young woman who had introduced him. She wore the same look of honest happiness.

"Mom. Oh Mom, what did you think?"

"Malcolm, I'm so proud. Your performance was beautiful. It was passionate. If only your father were still alive, he'd be so proud of you. I'm so proud…so proud. You really had the audience. They loved you and loved what you gave them."

"Ms. Hayes, wasn't he wonderful?" the girl said.

"Oh Mom, sorry, this is Riley."

"Pleased to meet you, Riley. Yes, he was wonderful, but of course, I'm partial."

Eve chuckled at the clichéd thing that parents always say.

"Ms. Hayes, I know Malcolm's too modest to tell you," Riley said, "but there was a representative from the Museum of Modern Art in New York in the audience. He wants to meet with Malcolm and talk about adding his show to their fall program."

"Jeepers. That's fantastic news," Eve said.

"Malcolm, have you told your mother about our other news?"

His grin changed to a look of trepidation. "No…no, I haven't." Malcolm was staring down at his shoes, hoping that his mother was not paying attention.

"What other news?"

"Tell her, Malcolm."

"Mom, Riley and I are engaged."

Eve stared straight at him. It was a deadpan stare of shock. She'd had no idea that he was even dating anyone.

"Engaged? Like marriage engaged? When were you going to tell me? Are you moving out? We just got the new house and you took the garage apartment."

Separation anxiety immediately welled up inside Eve. She felt more anguish from the thought of Malcolm leaving than she had when her husband passed away.

"We haven't set a date yet. Riley is moving in with me."

Eve was only slightly relieved, but still felt off-balance because her son, now engaged, might go to New York in the fall. She had to look at it for what it was. Her son was turning into an adult and doing adult things. Logically, she had to let Malcolm live his life, and show a face of approval and support. However, within the very rational Eve, no amount of logic could calm her emotions or dampen her motherly reactions. She forced herself to swallow it all down and let him go.

"I'm so happy for you two," Eve heard herself say. "Whatever you need from me, just let me know."

"Mom, there's a few of us going out tonight." Malcolm felt guilty and, though the offer was not sincere, he asked, "Do you want to join us?"

"I would love to, but I'm going to see a college friend's new house. Lucy will be there too."

Malcolm looked relieved and the happiness came back to his face. He grasped Riley's hand and looked over at the door, where a few twentysomethings were standing.

"Mom, our friends are about to leave."

"Go on, have a good time. Go celebrate. I'm supposed to be there in ten minutes. Her house is just a few blocks down, so I'm walking there."

She had always wanted to live on Rainbow Row. It was arguably the most photographed and painted landmark in the city. This small cluster of Caribbean-colored homes was over two hundred years old, and they were relics of the past, hardly ever up for sale. It was therefore not surprising that tiny drops of jealousy rained into Eve's thoughts. The house Diana and her husband had purchased was the yellow one, the one with indigo shutters. Eve knew that house well, had always liked it, and had naturally seen it in a thousand different paintings and watercolors. She had always been curious as to what the interior looked like, and now she would get her chance to find out.

When Diana opened the door she gave Eve a big hug, and though it was a warm and friendly embrace, it still made Eve uncomfortable. She stared down at the floor. It was the original oak planking, mended in a place or two, but it still looked great for its age. Diana showed her around and told her about the history of the old house, and even though she already knew in immense detail about the history of Diana's new home, Eve pretended not to.

The historical home, built in 1741, was originally a city house for a wealthy colonial planter who was prominent in early South Carolina politics. The house fell into disrepair after the Civil War, but underwent an expert renovation in the 1960s to correct earlier alterations before achieving its historical landmark status. A massive staircase leading up to the second and third floors dominated the grand entrance hall. The home was an architectural opus, highlighted by fine lines and ancient cypress railings that had turned a deep shade of black-brown over the years. Sparsely decorated, like the rest of the house, the foyer made the house look cavernous. Shiny white wainscoting under periwinkle walls enveloped the space, and this theme, carried down the hallway, tied into the back of the house. The paneled walls turned into the moving-box-filled living and dining rooms, and back out to the hallway, ending at the kitchen doorway.

Next to the kitchen was a large den, perhaps a music room in the past, since musical notes and symbols were painted on the periwinkle walls just below the crown molding. Diana and Jack had closed on the house the month before, and the den was the only room that Diana had had time to decorate. However, it missed the mark of the old and often stuffy design ethic that most of these homes had established as Charleston style. In one corner rested a weather-beaten oak drafting table. It was covered with color sketches of concert logos and band names, and on the right side sat a pile of T-shirt samples. A laptop sat on a narrow writing desk to the right of the drafting table.

Along one wall was a Napoli low cabinet with glass doors, its shelves filled with record albums. The worn edges of album sleeves, like a childhood recollection, were both familiar and strange to see in a digital era. Atop the cabinet was a stereo system with a turntable spinning an Edith Piaf record at thirty-three-and-a-third speed. The stereo was wedged between a pair of speakers oozing out "La Vie en Rose." An old Gibson acoustic guitar with a dark-brown sunburst rested in a guitar stand to the left of the cabinet. On the other side of the wall was a tall bookshelf with glass doors next to a leather wingback chair and a small table and reading lamp. A brown lap blanket was draped over the chair, making it like a small bed.

Two comfortable brown leather love seats formed an L in the center of the room, joined together by a rather nondescript end table. Angled just so, both love seats faced a tall bay window that overlooked a well-manicured courtyard lined with palmetto trees. The prickly palmettos were lit by dramatic lighting. All three of the open windows, raised high, let the sound of the cicadas waft in along with a cool evening breeze. It was here that Eve found Lucy, sitting and staring out the window drinking red wine.

"There you are, darling," Lucy said. She remained seated and motioned for Eve. "Come sit next to me. I'd get up, but I'm a bit tipsy. Mother always said being drunk is never a crime, but looking like you're drunk is criminal."

Diana laughed at the joke, but Eve only smiled. "Diana, is that your old guitar over there?" she asked.

"Yes. That's the first guitar I ever bought. My other guitars are in storage."

"You never forget your first," Lucy said.

Diana said, "Ha," but Eve only smiled. "It's the one I got when I went to Nashville with Maggie."

"Have you thought about performing again?" Eve asked.

"Well, sometimes it runs through my mind."

"Darling, you really should consider it," Lucy said. "Talent like yours should never go to waste."

"Thank you, Lucy. You know it's been a long time. Twenty years, and they've gone by so fast."

Diana readjusted her position and tucked her legs under her.

"We broke up in July of ninety-five. The only time we got back together was for a George Jones tribute later that year. I was pregnant with Samantha during that show and I haven't performed since. Unless you count singing for the kids at bedtime."

"And what about your kids? And Jack?" Eve asked. "When are they going to be here?"

"Another week. They're just about to wrap up school. Jack had to take care of some business matters. Can't wait to see them."

Next to Lucy was a bottle of wine and an empty glass. She poured a glass of wine and passed it to Eve.

"I know you don't drink red wine very often, but you just have to try this Rothschild Cab. Drink it in with your nose first."

"It's so good," Diana said.

Eve inhaled from the bell of the wineglass, but her thoughts seemed elsewhere.

"That is very nice. A strong aroma...but I have news."

"What is it, dear?" Lucy said.

"Malcolm's engaged."

"Hey, congratulations," Diana said.

Lucy looked shocked and her reply was more incredulous. "What? Malcolm? He's engaged? I had no idea he was even dating anyone."

"Me neither. First time I met her was tonight. Her name's Riley something or another."

"Wait, so you've never met her until tonight?" Diana asked.

"No. Malcolm has always been very private about everything, especially his love life."

"Well, I'm very surprised," Lucy said. "I always thought he was a lot like his father."

"What do you mean 'like his father'?" Eve asked.

"You know, not so much interested in dating, more into the arts, a little skittish when it came to girls."

"Eve, I'm curious," Diana said. "When did you get pregnant with Malcolm?"

"On our honeymoon, in fact it had to be that first night since it was the only time we had sex. Porter became ill with a stomach virus and nothing happened for the rest of the trip. When we returned home I realized I was pregnant."

Eve looked into the dark-crimson wine before taking a sip.

"I've never told anyone this, but after that first time, Porter and I never had intercourse again, he was...sporadically impotent. Occasionally I would, you know, kiss him down there."

"You mean a blow job?" Diana asked.

Eve blushed and a little grin began to curl up on her lips. "Yes, that."

"So you never had sex with your husband, except for that first time?" Diana asked.

"Nope."

"What about a lover? Surely you got your needs met somewhere else."

"Oh, come on, Diana. You know me. I'd never fool around like that."

"As a relationship expert, don't you find that strange?"

"Porter satisfied me in many other ways. He and I shared an intellectual bond. He helped guide my sense of style. He knew what I liked and would help me pick out my clothes and hairstyle. It's not just about a physical connection. Relationships based on sex do not last. We had a greater bond."

Diana's eyes were stuck in a position of astonishment.

"Wow, Eve, I couldn't do it, go without sex. I mean not have sex with my husband."

"Me either, darling," Lucy said. "I need to be satisfied and that's one thing Theo's a pro at."

"Eve, can I be candid?" Diana said.

"Yes."

"Do you remember that first summer when Porter came by the beach house?"

"Yes."

"Maggie told me she thought he was gay. During her first year at the college, she hung out with a couple of guys who said they knew him from the gay bars in Columbia. I never told you because I didn't know if it were true or not."

"My Porter, gay?"

Eve chugged her wine and passed it to Lucy for a refill. The bells had gone off in Eve's head so clearly, it forced her to face the truth about Porter and their sex life. She had often approached this thought during her early years with Porter, but excused the absence of sex as one of his quirks. Eve had also blamed herself, realizing that she was never a very sexual or romantic person and had put all of her energies into grad school and later, her professorship.

"I can't believe what I'm thinking now. My husband was gay."

The thought had quickly changed from a question to a statement of realization and the dumbfounded feeling that she should have known and seen it much earlier.

Lucy passed her the newly refilled wineglass and Eve chugged again.

"Darling, people say things about my cousin Randy," Lucy said. "You know him, the one who looks like Tom Cruise and owns the ad agency. He dates lots of pretty girls, and just because he's never married doesn't mean he's gay."

Eve was staring out the window, her eyes fixed on one point, and she passed her glass back to Lucy for another refill. "No, Lucy. My husband was gay. How could I not see it?"

It was as if Eve's eyes were stuck. She could not blink.

"His grad assistants were always male and he always took them to conferences that I never attended." Her mouth agape, Eve shook her head from time to time. "Did you know he would take me shopping and put together outfits for me? His clothing was always more expensive than mine. One time we were watching an old movie and the scene took place in the bedroom of a married couple. They had two twin beds and he pointed it out to me as something that interested him. He would tell me how glamorous I was, but never even touched my breast."

A sad laughter came out of her throat.

"When I told him I was a virgin, he told me he was too. I married a gay man. Gay, gay, gay."

Eve again took the wine down in one swallow. Diana and Lucy were astonished and didn't know what to say.

"Diana, do you have any pot?" Eve asked. "I'd like to waltz in Vienna right now."

From out of one of the cabinets, Diana produced her red dragon box. In the background Edith Piaf launched into "Non, Je Ne Regrette Rein." For the first time in her life, regret filled Eve to the brim. Diana lit the joint and passed it to Eve. This time she inhaled it down into her lungs without coughing. She held the herbaceous smoke in her lungs until she released it with a deep exhalation. After this joint, a second went round and round and the three women were stoned.

"I feel like a fraud," Eve said. "I give out relationship advice on the radio, I've written articles and books about the importance of pragmatism in relationships. Yet my deceased husband, who was twenty years older than me, was gay. I've only had sex one time...once...just one time. To top it all off, tonight my son tells me he's engaged to a woman that I just met for the first time. Does anyone else see the irony?"

"Oh, come on, Eve," Diana said. "You're still young. You're smart and beautiful. You need to live a little and put yourself out there."

"That's so sweet of you, Diana, but I don't know about that. It's too late for romance with a woman in her forties. I wish I had been like you and Maggie when we were in college. Heck, I'm practically a virgin."

"Darling, don't be so hard on yourself," Lucy said.

Eve was holding her glass of wine, staring at it.

"That's easy for you to say, Lucy. You have a handsome and passionate husband who loves you, and makes love to you. He's a very devoted man who works very hard for you and your sons. And you, Diana, I've only met him once, but Jack has to be the sweetest man I've ever met. I can tell he's still madly in love with you."

Eve drank a little wine, and unconsciously swirled the wine around in her glass.

"I need to go to the bathroom," Eve said. "Which way is it?"

"It's the door across from the dining room."

Feeling more than tipsy, Eve tried to stand up, but fell backward into the overstuffed loveseat. As she did her wineglass tipped backward, causing the crimson liquid to fly up into the air and land on her white sweater.

"Jeepers! What else can go wrong?"

"It's okay, it's okay," Diana said. "Let's get you cleaned up."

"Don't feel bad, Eve," Lucy said. "I've done it myself."

Diana was quickly to her feet and made a beeline for the kitchen. She came back in an instant with a dishtowel and passed it to Eve, who immediately began blotting her sweater.

"Aw fudge, this is my favorite sweater."

"Honey, it can be cleaned," Lucy said. She got up and grabbed the blanket from the leather chair by the bookshelf. "Here, take off your sweater. Your bra too, and wrap yourself up in this blanket."

Lucy had Eve's clothes in her hand. "Diana, I need hot water and a good amount of salt. It's the best thing for a wine stain." Lucy spoke from experience.

"Salt's in the cabinet above the stove, help yourself." Lucy left for the kitchen. "Come on upstairs and let's find you something to wear."

A large walnut king-size sleigh bed dominated the master bedroom. Despite the antique bed's plain design based on simple lines, the wood grain was highly figured, making it a warm invitation to the art of sleeping beautifully. On the wall, facing the foot of the bed, was a matching lowboy chest of drawers with a large mirror hanging above it.

To the left of the bed were two large windows, draped in cream-colored sheers, that overlooked the rear of the house. Squatting in front of the windows was a pair of plush cream-colored chairs that shared a small reading table. A door nearby opened to a small Juliet balcony.

While most old homes such as this rarely have closets in their bedrooms, much less an en suite bathroom, the previous owner had expanded into another bedroom and created a small but luxurious bathroom and walk-in closet. Diana's clothes filled most of the closet, and on a rack of mostly blue jeans and blouses, she thumbed through a small section of dresses and pulled out a black wrap dress.

"I know we're not the same size, but this should fit you if we cinch it in the waist."

Eve undressed in the master bathroom and slipped into the black dress. As was to be expected, Diana's knee-length dress was well above Eve's knees and, cut for Diana's larger figure, hung loose and free. Diana pulled the dress around Eve's much thinner frame and tightened it with the matching belt.

"There," Diana said, "it looks lovely on you."

It was twelve thirty by the time Eve called it a night and walked back to her car. She was very stoned, higher than she had ever been. Lucy had gone home earlier, leaving Eve and Diana to have one last waltz in Vienna. The moon over Rainbow Row hung like a Chinese lantern in a cobalt-blue sky. Eve could clearly see the muted colors and architectural nuances of the antebellum homes.

The air was different from when she'd first arrived. A northeast breeze had freshened and spilled across the bay, and the wind tossed around her usually straight and coifed blond hair. Disheveled, it suited her better than the hairstyle she had had for years. She felt alive as the cool air slipped into the loose-fitting dress and titillated her skin.

The gravity of the evening's events and life realizations did not matter anymore. Eve surprisingly felt free from what she believed was expected of her. As a young girl, she'd spent her days placating her father and mother. He had been a psychiatrist with a disdain for popular culture, she a dentist fixated on body image. The sum of these parental influences and their "professional" marriage had served as the bedrock for Eve's outlook on relationships and marriage. She'd become an advocate for common sense in love and romance. Tonight she questioned that premise, questioned the validity of her own marriage, and reconsidered the meanings of love and romance.

A block away from the theater, she stopped for a moment and studied her reflection in the storefront window of a bakery that appeared locked up for the night. In the amber hue of the streetlights, she saw someone who looked like her, but it was a woman with tousled hair wearing a revealing dress, and she liked that woman. She wanted to be that woman.

At the top of the window, green, white, and red lettering read "Giovanni's Pasticceria." Just behind the window was a refrigerated display case replete with pastries, cakes, and desserts.

For years she had gone by this bakery, and like many of the other shops surrounding it, to her it was nothing more than a part of the streetscape. It was not a place where she would have stopped, let alone shopped. Until now the thought of a slice of cake, a chocolate confection, a petit four, or even a cream cheese croissant had not appealed to her. It was not because she did not like the taste of such things—admittedly, she had never tried them—but her sugar phobia had created a fear of what they would do to her slim figure and pearly white teeth.

Euphoria is that beautiful effect marijuana has on the human mind. It manifests itself in many ways and one of them is in the joy of eating. Eve had often felt a twinge of unabashed hunger after waltzing in Vienna. To be sure, she had witnessed Diana and Lucy tear through bags of chips or boxes of powdered donuts, or down a whole canister of Betty Crocker chocolate icing. Once she'd even witnessed the very vegetarian Maggie Bloomer dip her morning biscuit in bacon fat. Nevertheless, she had always been able to control herself.

Tonight it was all very different and she was stoned like never before. She had missed dinner for Malcolm's show and had a serious case of the munchies. Standing in front of the bakery window, she felt her curiosity piqued by the pink petit fours, and the chocolate cake charmed her. As with Pavlov's dog, the bell was ringing and she was salivating.

As she stared through the plate-glass window, she noticed movement in the back of the bakery. At first it was a blur of white and khaki, but once her eyes refocused, she saw a swarthy man with dark hair kneading a curved mass of dough. He was massaging it passionately, stretching and caressing it with his thick arms and broad hands. A thin layer of flour covered his white t-shirt and khaki pants. Broad-shouldered and thick, the man was the antithesis of Porter and she could see his five o'clock shadow (from two days ago) framing his sun-bronzed face.

Eve's appetite changed, and her eyes and thoughts shifted from the sweet pastries to him. She watched him knead the soft white dough, squeezing and stretching until it became limber and supple. While one massive hand held the dough, the other grabbed a handful of flour and thrust it toward the dough in a burst of white. She watched him subdue the dough and gently lay it down on the wooden working table.

The man turned and spotted Eve watching him. He smiled and gave a little wave of his hand. While grabbing a towel to wipe his hands, he walked to the front door of the bakery.

"I'm so sorry, miss, we closed," he said.

His deep voice was made lyrical by his thick Italian accent.

The feeling Eve experienced was unfamiliar to her. It was the same feeling a teenage girl has when she comes face-to-face with a boy she has had a crush on from afar. That momentary speechless and dumbfounded moment when she realizes he is talking to her.

"Oh. Okay, of course."

Eve stood frozen, staring at him, feeling a dumb smile on her face that she could not stop, did not want to stop.

"Miss, you need something? You okay?"

"I'm okay. I saw your desserts and I was…uh…thought they looked delicious."

"You want to try them? Come in. I let you sample some things. Okay?"

"Really?"

"Yes."

Inside the bakery, an atmosphere heavy with the smells of sweet cakes, pastries, and confections greeted Eve. Maria Callas sang opera in the background and the warm air of the bakery reverberated with her rendition of Violetta's aria from *La Traviata*. There was an ambiance in this little bakery. The sugary smells, the amber lighting, and Callas's voice caught in a passionate lament caused Eve's head to spin. It was all so divine, like some other time or place where all the senses unite in perfect harmony.

To the left was a long refrigerated case of pastries and cakes. A counter extended from the case to the back of the wall. Behind the refrigerated case was a rustic wooden rack with baskets that were empty cradles waiting for freshly baked breads. To the right of the baskets was a stack of commercial ovens. Built into the back corner, a woodburning oven gave off a pleasing warmth and aroma. Between the ovens stood a large wooden worktable where the soft mound of dough was reclining after its workout.

On the opposite side of the bakery were a dozen café tables with chairs arranged like paired dancers. The space was enveloped by the exposed brick walls, part of the original structure and built over a century ago.

He motioned for Eve to come with him behind the counter, and, grabbing a nearby stool, he planted it along the kitchen side of the counter. With a polite wave of his hand, he offered her the seat. "One moment, please."

Grabbing a towel, he opened one of the ovens and deftly removed a tray of miniature pastry shells. He slid the hot baking pan into a nearby cooling rack.

"Fruit tarts tomorrow," he said.

He reached out to shake Eve's hand.

"My name is Giovanni Panini, but call me Gio, everybody does."

Eve nodded her head in agreement. "Gio. Okay."

There was a pause as he waited for her to introduce herself, but she did not. A big grin replaced his pleasant smile. "And *signora*, your name is?"

Eve laughed, not having realized how long the pause had been since she'd last spoken.

"My name? I'm sorry, of course, it's Eve Greene. Hayes. I mean Eve Hayes."

"So are you Greene or Hayes?"

"My maiden name was Greene, but I'm Eve Hayes."

"Oh, you are married?"

"No, a widow."

"I'm so sorry," he said.

"It's okay. Really, it's okay. He died over a year ago, but after what I realized tonight, maybe he was gone long before then, maybe never really there."

Eve looked back at the world she'd thought she lived in, and became quiet. Confusion gripped her and she realized how painfully clueless she had been during her almost twenty years of marriage.

Gio was puzzled by this but could say nothing except, "I'm so sorry."

She looked at him and thought how friendly his face looked. The lines on his tanned face were like roads on a map, all leading to his jovial character and sincere brown eyes. She immediately felt relaxed, and she smiled back at him.

"So, tell me what you do, Eve Greene Hayes."

"I'm a professor at the College of Charleston. Psychology department. What about you? Italian, right?"

"Yes, originally I come from Bologna, *Italia*, but now I am American."

"And how long have you been here?"

"Eighteen years now. I first came on a work visa, as marine engineer at Norfolk shipyard in Virginia. That's where I met my ex-wife, she was engineer too."

"Ah, so you were married? How long?"

"Seven years," he said. "One day I come home from work and she was in bed with the boss of the company. In one moment, wife gone, job gone, house gone. After that one moment, I take my savings, buy a sailboat, and plan to sail away from big mess. Maybe I sail to nowhere, maybe Caribbean island, maybe return to *Italia*, I don't know at this time, you see."

"So how did you end up here?"

"I make sail under perfect weather when I leave Portsmouth. It was high tide, moderate seas under steady breezes. Perfect sailing weather. I make bearing southwesterly pointed to Bahamas. Soon weather change and oncoming tropical storm forces me to take harbor in Charleston. I tell myself to stay until weather is better."

"And how long ago was that?" she asked.

"That was a little over ten years ago. So, the next day, beautiful sunrise and I go for walk around this charming city and ask myself why I am running away? She should not be a reason to run from life. So I decide to make my boat my home and look for a job. After a few weeks, the space in this building became available and I use the rest of my savings to start this bakery. At first, selling simple rustic breads my mother taught me when I was little boy."

"And do you still live on the boat?"

"Yes. It is where I sleep," he said, "but I am here most of the day and night, every day except Sunday out of respect for the *Padre*."

The music changed and Maria Callas launched into the overture from *Carmen*.

"Oh wait, I forget. I offer for you to try my desserts."

"What would you recommend?"

"What do you like? Chocolates? Pastries? Cakes?"

"I don't know. I've never tried any of them before. Never had cake, I'm sad to say."

"*O mio Dio*. You kidding me, right? You never had cake?"

"No, never. I've always avoided sugar. I used to know why, but I can't remember now." Eve laughed.

"Okay, I got something for you," he said.

When the door to the refrigerated case hinged open Eve felt the chilled air drift out. The cool air was a dessert itself, sweetened by the cakes and pies that rested within. Carefully he lifted out a dark and rich chocolate cake. The cake had a few portions already cut out, and waxed paper inserts covered the open ends. From under the counter, he pulled out a plate and fork, and after removing the waxed paper, he used a knife to cut off a generous portion of the cake, gently laying it down on the plate and presenting it to Eve.

"*Torta al cioccolato.* Everybody loves chocolate cake."

Eve picked up the fork and probed it like a little kid given a plate of broccoli and unsure about taking that first bite. She slid her fork into the cake and picked out a small bite from the dark rich center, avoiding the icing. She slowly brought the fork to her smiling lips. At first a small taste. She suddenly released a quick and sensual breath of surprise. It was at that moment that Eve's senses of taste and smell awoke from forty years of dormancy. She shoved the rest of the cake on her fork into her mouth and the flavors of chocolate and sugar captivated her.

"Oh, that's good. That is so…so good. I never thought I'd like it. Wow, just wow."

Gio pulled another fork from under the counter and scooped up an oversize forkful of cake with icing.

"Try some with icing, in one bite."

She was laughing, and her mouth was wide open. Gio fed her the cake and she took the whole bite, filling her mouth with the sweet chocolate cake and rich icing. She laughed from the pure joy of chocolate.

"So good…so good. I want more, more, more."

He fed her the rest of the cake as fast as she could eat it.

Eve's sense of focus was slowly coming back to her. She found Gio incredibly interesting. He was a bear of a man, large and broad, but calm and warm. He made her feel relaxed and she immediately felt comfortable in his presence.

"You want more to try?" he asked.

Eve nodded her head. She wanted more and she wanted Gio to give it to her. He reached into the case, removed two lovely pink petit fours, and placed them on a plate.

"Now, you try this, petit fours *alla confettura di fragole*…strawberry petit fours."

Eve went to take the plate from him, but he pulled it back.

"No, I will feed them to you."

"Okay," she said.

A very delighted Eve leaned back on the stool and stretched out her long legs, causing Diana's black dress to rise up even higher along her creamy white thighs. Her reclined pose loosened the belted waist, causing the front of the dress to open and reveal her rarely exposed cleavage.

The first pink petit four to hit her red lips was silky smooth. She bit into the cake and the sweet scent of strawberries tickled her nose in concert with the flavors on her tongue. He fed the second pink morsel to her, but her appetite was more insatiable than before.

"More, I want more."

For a big man he made a graceful turn and slid the

door of the display case open, grabbing a plate of pastries.

"This is struffoli. Fried pastry balls with honey."

He placed one into her mouth and she crunched down, savoring the sticky honey. He tossed the plate down on the counter and grabbed a cookie-filled plate from the case.

"Chestnut tortelli. I cover mine with powdered sugar."

Gio picked up one of the snowy-white crescents and placed it into Eve's mouth. The rush of sugar was rapturous and she grabbed another one and placed it into his mouth as he moved closer to her. Powdered sugar covered her right hand, making it look like five sweet ladyfinger desserts. He grabbed her hand, looked her into her eyes, and kissed her sugarcoated fingers.

With her cravings for sweets satisfied, a new desire came over her mind and body. She was aware of the effects of being aroused, knew them more from her clinical studies than from firsthand experience. There was the tingling sensation, the immediate warmth and flush to her face. Her breathing became rapid, and she wanted this man, a man she barely knew, to touch her, kiss her, and press his body against hers.

"More, I want more," she said.

Her voice was breathy and she was clearly aroused.

Gio's face was flushed with excitement as much as Eve's. His chest broadened from deep passionate breaths. In a rush he grabbed a container from the dessert case.

"This is zabaglione. It is custard, sweet, creamy, smooth. I make with Marsala wine."

He stared into her eyes and hers fixed on his.

Dipping his fingers into the creamy custard, he touched her lips and she kissed him, licking the creaminess from his fingers. He pulled her close to him and their custard-glazed lips met in a deeply passionate kiss. Locked into a dessert-induced embrace, they shifted their position toward the low wooden worktable. His broad arm pushed the dough to the side as he laid her backward on the flour-covered table. They kissed, and he touched her, held her, and caressed her.

After years of self-control, she surrendered to raw passion. Her inhibitions were replaced by an immediate desire for this man to take her and caress her body as he had the soft dough. Tonight, more than anytime in her life, she needed someone to want her as a woman. She wished that he would lust after her and become aroused because she was woman and he was a man. Tonight she got her wish.

WALTZING in VIENNA

~10~

EVE'S HOUSE

L ucy pulled her Mercedes sedan along the curb of Lee Street in front of the manicured lawns of the Citadel parade ground. Even though it was Saturday afternoon on a mild summer day, the campus was particularly active, and a broad warm breeze caused the great trees on the south end to sway back and forth. The old walkways had seen the heels of many boots over the years, and today they carried young cadets in their leave uniforms, accompanied by their girlfriends, to and from campus.

In the back of the car, Lucy's twin sons were in their dress grays, made identical by the conformity of their perfect uniforms. They were well-built young men just like their father. Strong square chins served as foundations for their broad down-turned lips and straightforward noses, on faces punctuated by deep-set dark eyes. A reddish tan on their faces and necks told the story of all the drills, marches, and training they had received during their first year as cadets at the Citadel.

Teddy and William quietly exited the car from the backseat, and placed their hats squarely on their heads. Automatically standing at attention, as if it had been called for by their commanding officer, they stood upright facing their mother's car, waiting for her to dismiss them from their lunch date with her. Lucy lowered the window and leaned out to them, smiling like a mother sending her young boys off to elementary school.

William broke attention and stepped forward to the open car window. "Thank you for lunch, Mother."

It was a monotonous delivery, from his expressionless cadet face, but Lucy could see a sparkle in his eyes, the same sparkle he'd had when he was younger and would grin at her. Teddy just nodded.

"You're welcome, boys."

Her smile flattened with the realization that they were boys no longer. She'd was going to tell them she loved them, but she said nothing. William paused, waiting for her to say what she did not say, but he stepped back from the car after that moment of silence.

Teddy gave William a little punch on the shoulder, as if to say, "Let's move on," and then the two turned and walked toward one of the massive buildings. She gave a little sigh, pulled her car away from the curb, and pointed it down the street, heading for the city center.

Lucy tapped the switch on the radio and turned to her favorite oldies radio station. She caught the last bit of an Alanis Morissette song before a deep-voiced female DJ piped up. "That was 'Ironic' by Alanis Morissette from her album *Jagged Little Pill*. This is

WOCN, Ocean Radio, Charleston, South Carolina. Up next I've got Sheryl Crow, Natalie Merchant, and Tori Amos as we chart female rockers of the nineties. First up, one of Charleston's very own, the Crazy Hearts. Hey, I wonder whatever happened to them, they were such a great girl group. Here they are with their song 'Chase the Sun' from way back in 1994."

A drum intro quietly began the song, sounding like the syncopated rhythm of a train on a long track. As the lonesome rhythm built, slide guitar slipped down around a minor scale and the bass came in, quietly doubling the downbeat of the drums.

I used to dream, used to dream
I used to dream so far away
'Bout going far, going far
About going to distant lands

You used to say, used to say
You used to say you'd take me there
But now you got, now you got
You got my love clutched in your hands

Before Diana's voice drifted off and the chorus started, a drum fill propelled a grungy guitar riff that sounded like Kurt Cobain meets Chet Atkins.

That's why I want, why I want
I want to leave this place real soon
We'll ride all day, ride all night
We'll chase the sun and raise the moon

Nanananana
Nananananay

Nanananana
Nananananay

The song backed off and returned to its quiet, lonesome feel, like a train running along a line late at night.

We used to ride, used to ride
Would ride all the day and night
We'd go to places, to places
We'd go to places far away

But now we stay, now we stay
Now we stay just the way we are
Never changing, not changing
And now it's all fading away

The second chorus broke in with the drum roll and grungy guitar riff:

That's why I want, why I want
I want to leave this place real soon
We'll ride all day, ride all night
We'll chase the sun and raise the moon

Nanananana
Nananananay
Nanananana
Nananananay

After college Lucy had rarely listened to top forty or rock radio, and her recollection of great music was of classical music and opera performed in Charleston's concert halls, or the sacred music performed in church. There were some memories of Diana's band, and though she remembered hearing this song, she had never paid attention to the lyrics. They were the words of a twentysomething woman singing about change and freedom, and to Lucy's middle-aged mind, they sounded so foreign. It was hard to imagine that the singer was her old friend, and since Lucy could separate the Diana of today from the young woman singing the song, she realized how talented Diana truly was. Lucy especially liked the line "We'll chase the sun and raise the moon." It gave her a little lift in her spirit, and the idea of going somewhere seemed so freeing, even though they were the words of a person and time so far away.

Along the narrow streets, she passed sun-glazed tourists wearing their summer clothes, hats, and sunglasses. Some of them were lost, staring with confusion at hotel guide maps, while some were pointing to this house or that church. The ubiquitous horse-drawn carriages were out in force today, the horses clopping and snapping their hooves down on the pavement as passengers listened to facts about the city from the young drivers.

She wound her way down a one-way street in one of the smaller neighborhoods with smallish homes. A few blocks more and she stopped in front of a small one-story cottage painted Wedgwood blue with white trim. It had a very clean yard by Charleston standards. Neatly trimmed crape myrtles were on each side of the yard, like parentheses, while bloomless azaleas lined the road's edge and encircled the house. Although they are never the first choice for topiary, the azaleas looked more like low coping than a living plant.

Two cars parked side by side filled what little driveway had been carved out of the front yard, so Lucy had to park on the street and wait for a carriage to pass by before stepping out. She locked her doors and walked around to an entrance framed by the low azalea wall. The walk up to the house was made of very old bricks, ancient bricks that carried her up to the front door of the house, but before she could ring the bell, Eve opened the door. Lucy looked strangely at her. There was something different about Eve, something she did not understand. Perhaps she was wearing a new dress. It was a simple summer dress. Done in bright yellow, it seemed to make her otherwise pale skin look browner than usual. This, combined with a plunging neckline, and the fact that she was not wearing a bra, made for a look that was not what Lucy would have expected of her.

Eve gave her a welcoming smile and laughed for no reason, a happy laugh. "Hi, Lucy," Eve said. "Sorry, but we already started smoking."

"That's okay, dear. My lunch with the boys ran late."

Eve swung to one side and gestured Lucy into the house with a wave of her hand. "Diana's brought a bottle of Pinot. We were just about to open it."

Eve's small cottage was sparse. Along the wall opposite the front window sat a Biedermeier sofa covered by an ivory-colored fabric in contrast with the dark mahogany frame. To the side was a large and well-worn end table, even darker than the mahogany of the sofa. It supported a modern-looking lamp made of glass and silver. The gangly lamp was out of proportion with everything else. Next to this was a large cream-colored wingback chair, well worn by the numerous nights Eve had sat in it during her frequent bouts with insomnia.

There were no rugs on the floor, and very few decorative items on the walls, save for a series of three black-and-white photographs of Eve holding Malcolm when he was a baby. There were no pictures of Porter anywhere in the house. His old desk and bookshelf that Lucy remembered from the other house were nowhere in sight. It was a clean and sparse house and the bare hardwood floors, polished to such a luster, reflected the incoming sunshine like wood-colored mirrors.

The two friends walked through the house, past the two bedrooms and eat-in kitchen, and out into the sun-room. It was one of those porches from an earlier time, now glassed in from floor to ceiling. Over the windows white sheers draped down, letting the light in, but the shrouds still provided privacy from the neighbors to the rear.

Against the wall, facing the window, was a little wicker love seat, bordered by two massive wicker chairs, one on each side. In the center was a big square coffee table made of dark slate. On top of this dark slate table were three empty wineglasses, Diana's red dragon box, a cigarette case, and a silver lighter.

Diana was in one of the big wicker chairs, slowly twisting the corkscrew into the top of the bottle of wine. She had a joint dangling from the corner of her mouth. With a muffled pop she removed the cork. As soon as she saw Lucy, she jumped up and put the bottle down, grabbing the half-burned joint and thrusting it out to Lucy.

"Hey, we just started this. Take a puff."

Lucy looked a little off-balance, but took the joint

anyway. "Thank you, darling."

She smiled and took a deep drag as Diana slipped back into her chair. Eve sat down in the love seat and Lucy took the other big wicker chair next to her. She passed the joint to Eve.

"So, what do you think about our girl Eve?" Diana asked.

Eve inhaled deeply from the joint, blew out a large plume of smoke, and laughed.

"What? Am I missing something?" Lucy asked.

"Well, look at her," Diana said. "Someone has the glow."

Eve passed the joint to Lucy and she inhaled the silky smoke before passing it to Diana. She looked at Eve and studied her face and form. Was it the dress? Maybe it was a new hairstyle. In the cooler light of the porch, she could see that Eve's complexion was darker than the perky pale face she had always known. She looked softer, warmer, and more inviting.

"Eve, have you gained weight since we last saw you?"

Diana burst out laughing, almost rolling out of her chair. "No, no, she has the glow."

Lucy finally got the meaning of what Diana was saying. In her realization she gasped. "Eve, do you have a man?"

She did not answer at first. Her cheeks blushed to match the red wine she was quietly pouring into the three glasses. She took a deep breath, followed by a sweet sigh, and gave a wink and a sly smile.

"Yes," Eve said, "and I have gained a few pounds."

"She hasn't told me a thing yet." Diana said. "She said she wouldn't until you got here.

Lucy leaned forward. "I'm so happy for you, Eve. Who it is? Professor Barnes? Dr. Davis?"

"Neither," Eve said.

Eve stretched her back and cracked her neck by leaning her head back. She lit another joint, pausing just enough to tease the girls with anticipation.

"Okay, are you ready for me to tell you?" She took a drag and passed it to Lucy. "After the last time we got together at Diana's house it was late when I walked back to my car, and on the way back I passed that little Italian bakery, Giovanni's. You know, I've been by that place so many times and never paid much attention to it, but this time I stopped to check out all of the sweet stuff in the front window."

"Oh yeah, just down from my house," Diana said. "I love the cannoli there."

Eve took the joint as it came around, puffing on it before continuing her story.

"Now, y'all know I've never had what you call the munchies, but that night I was so hungry. I wanted to eat all of it. I pictured myself smashing the window, grabbing everything, and running back to my car. I was lusting over the food until I saw the owner in the back kneading this big mound of dough. He's—"

A pounding on the back door interrupted Eve.

"Oh fuck," Eve said, "who could that be?"

"Should I put away the pot?" Diana asked.

"Let me see who it is first," Eve said.

She jumped up and walked through a small mudroom. A minute later she came back through the porch and walked past Lucy and Diana.

"Who was it, dear?" Lucy asked.

"Malcolm," she said, calling out from the hallway, "he wants to borrow my car."

She came back with keys in hand and went out through the mudroom. A few minutes later she returned to her seat.

"Where was I?" Eve asked.

"You were telling us about how you wanted to smash the window until you saw a man with a bunch of dough," Diana said.

"Oh yeah, the owner of the bakery. I was just staring at him and he saw me watching him so he comes to the door. His name is Giovanni and he invited me in and asked if I want to sample some things. So I said yes. Oh my God, it smelled so good in there. He likes opera, and the place is so quaint. It's got that classic Italian feel, you know, like *Lady and the Tramp*, little checkered tablecloths and pictures of Frank Sinatra on the wall."

"Eve," Diana said, "enough about how the bakery looked, tell us what happened."

"Well, he invited me behind the counter and I tried chocolate cake at first, I loved that. He fed me petit fours, some kind of honey pastry, and this real creamy Italian custard. Hey, did you know that the croissant is not actually French, he told me it's originally from Vienna. How funny is that?"

"Eve," Diana said again, "what happened? Surely you're not blushing from eating dessert. Come on and tell us."

"Oh. Yeah, I was sampling some things and he started feeding me and," Eve said with a pause, "we started kissing. Then, you know, we got kind of crazy."

"Way to go, Eve," Diana said, "banging in the bakery." Diana was laughing hysterically.

"Did you, Eve?" Lucy asked with a big and

knowing grin.

"No, not there, but we almost got to that point. Gio stopped and said that was no way to start a relationship. He said he liked me and out of respect for me, we should stop."

Diana grimaced and spoke up. "Uh-oh, coitus interruptus. *Like* and *respect* are not things to say when you are getting it on with someone. So, are you two still friends?"

"Oh God, Diana, you're so awful," Lucy said. "Let Eve tell her story."

"It's okay, Lucy. I get it, but there's more. The following Sunday he invited me out on his sailboat."

"Darling, you on a boat?" Lucy said. "You are a natural swimming in the water, just not floating on top of it. Don't you remember when we were kids and Daddy took us fishing? You threw up the whole time."

"Didn't get sick at all. It was so beautiful, we sailed around the harbor and he made dinner for me. There was lasagna, and tiramisu for dessert. We ate it on deck and shared a bottle of wine, and the moon was huge. It was so romantic."

"And did you rock the boat after dinner?" Diana asked.

The grin on Eve's face was from ear to ear and a touch of crimson flushed her cheeks. "Yes, we did, over and over again."

"Are you still seeing him?" Lucy asked.

"Yes, I've been out on his boat three times now and the bakery most nights."

"So, is this serious?" Diana asked.

"I like him, and I think he likes me. We've been learning more and more about each other."

Eve lit up another joint, took a drag, and passed it to Diana.

"He's so passionate about his food. That and sailing. He's been testing recipes on me, stuff he may add to the bakery menu, perhaps even turn it into a true restaurant, a trattoria as he calls it."

When the joint came back around to Eve, she took a deep drag and held it. She kept on talking while holding her breath.

"Gio's even asked me to get involved," she said, gasping. "He'd run the kitchen and me the dining room and operations."

"That does sound serious," Lucy said.

"I know, I'd have to quit work, but I'm very serious about this."

"I'm so happy for you, darling," Lucy said.

"Me too," Diana said, "A little loving is a good thing. As they say in Italy, *la dolce vita*."

"Gio says that all of the time. I get it now, I really do."

The Pinot went down very well as Eve told them more about Gio.

"He's been teaching me how to work the boat too. Now I can work a halyard and hoist a sail. Did you know you adjust a sail by trimming it and you trim it by sheeting it?"

Diana and Lucy smiled at Eve's delighted grin. She was snickering at her description of sailing terminology, and how funny it all sounded.

"Bull sheet," Diana said.

"No sheet," Eve said, laughing.

Lucy was amazed to see her old friend so very happy. Of course, she had seen Eve laugh and smile, be satisfied and even happy over the years, but not like this. The laughter in Eve's voice was lyrical and filled with pure joy. Though Lucy would never have admitted it, nor was she conscious of it, jealousy filled her thoughts.

"This past Sunday was so beautiful. Porpoises swam alongside the boat and when the wind started up, he let me take the wheel for the first time. I steered the boat in front of the wind and even though he had his arms around me, helping me, I could feel the boat scream from beneath the waves. It was such a rush."

Diana and Lucy could see that Eve was falling in love. There was no mention from her about pragmatic relationships. She did not preach to them that relationships should be partnerships. No. Instead Eve spoke of passion and romance and of how he excited her. She spoke of food, and love, and how the senses must be pleased for one to feel alive. For the first time in over forty years, she was truly happy.

They talked about other things. Eve told them about Malcolm's girlfriend Riley Gadsden, and their plans for her to move in the next weekend. She told them about an awkward dinner they'd all had with Riley's parents. The dinner had been to celebrate the engagement of their children, but Riley's father, the very Reverend Gadsden, spent the whole evening hemming and hawing about their impending cohabitation. However, Eve, in her passion-induced state, was happy for them. She was at peace with their decision to move in together.

Lucy tipped the last of the wine into her glass and quoted *Oliver Twist* in an overemphasized English accent. "Please sir, I want some more."

"The Dickens you say," Diana said.

"But no Oliver twist-off bottles, please sir." Lucy chuckled.

"Yeah, yeah," Eve said. "Y'all are so punny. Let me go grab another bottle."

When Eve returned, she sat down, placed the bottle between her legs, and removed the cork.

"You know I could make a joke about that?" Diana said. "You know, *cork screw* and all."

Lucy was laughing at their banter and held her glass out. "Come on, just pour the damned wine," she said.

"Hold your ponies," Eve said. She poured out a large glass for Lucy and topped off her glass and Diana's.

"Oh. I haven't told you," Diana said. "I've lined up a gig playing at a bar in the Market next month."

"That's wonderful," Lucy said. "Where at?"

"Someplace called Café Ninety-Nine."

"Oh yeah," Eve said. "Lucy, that's where Rhett's Place used to be."

"How wonderful, Diana. Of course Eve and I will be there. What are the dates?"

"July ninth and tenth, in the evening from eight till ten," Diana said. "It's only for a hundred bucks a night, but I thought what the hell. I've been itching to perform again and since I'm back in the town where it all began, I ought to give it another chance."

"Oh, that's soon," Eve said. "I can bring Gio. I know he would love to come."

"Will Jack be there, Diana?"

"Yes."

"Fantastic," Lucy said. "I can't wait to meet him."

"Y'all are going to just love Gio. He's such a passionate man," Eve said.

The experiences of just a couple of weeks had reshaped Eve's view of love and romance. It was her new opinion that romance was capricious and spontaneous. It could grow anywhere and the divine spark could ignite the passions of the most dissimilar of people. Love obeyed no boundaries. It was fluid and took the shape of different people living in different circumstances. To try to control it would only destroy it.

Eve's story had inspired Lucy. For too long she had been complacent about her husband's frequent business trips, some lasting for weeks at a time. They rarely saw each other, but it was different from when they were first in love, when they had such passion that they could not wait to see one another.

Lucy and Theo had been spontaneous during the dawn of their relationship. It began like a nineteenth-century romance novel. She was a well-to-do young lady of society who found herself in the throes of a family tragedy, and he was the dashing officer who swept in and lifted her back to her feet. It was a passionate love at first. Straight from the pages of a romance novel.

Back then Theo would have done anything for her and cast off everything for a chance to see her. Like the time when she was on vacation with her mother and aunt Catherine in Hawaii. She and Theodore were getting very serious while he was stationed on Parris Island. He planned a surprise visit. He lied to Captain Hensley, his commanding officer, claiming that a family member was seriously ill. The captain granted Lieutenant Pendleton emergency leave without hesitation. From plane to plane he flew across the continental United States, and eventually he landed at the US Marine Corps base in Hawaii at Kaneohe Bay. Theodore, wearing his marine uniform, hitched rides across the island to where Lucy, her mother, and her aunt were staying, and, after arriving at the hotel, hired a carriage and asked the concierge to call her down to the lobby. He was waiting for her: he bowed down to her in that old style and presented her with a bouquet of pink sweetheart roses before they boarded the carriage for a slow tour of the hotel grounds. They had only one day to spend together before he had to get back on a transport plane and fly back to Parris Island.

It was a memory she had not thought about for some time. Indeed, there were many memories of love and passion between them, moments she'd thought she would always cherish, but had somehow pushed aside. Because of the freshness of her friend's romantic adventure, Lucy could clearly see the tenuous state of her marriage. A pang in her heart woke up her passion and all that she hoped for at this moment was for him to be at home tonight when she returned. Of course, that could not be, because last weekend he had flown back to Paris to oversee the finishing work on the new hotel. He would be gone for several weeks.

Since he would not return home for almost three weeks, Lucy decided she needed to be spontaneous too. She made up her mind that she would fly to Paris after Diana's show and surprise Theodore. Perhaps, she thought, they would drive down to the Bordeaux region once his work was complete and turn it into a romantic vacation. It was something she knew they both needed, a sudden burst of love and passion to reinvigorate their marriage.

WALTZING in VIENNA

~ 11 ~

ART OF PERFORMANCE

Through the driver's window of Diana's car and just over the harbor, dark clouds were visible blowing toward the city. The wind had picked up speed, swirling dust and leaves along the road. Flickers of distant lightning lit up the dark eastern horizon as a prelude to the oncoming storm. For Diana the rain was inviting, and in fact, she reveled in the sound of the rain. She had just started the car and was sitting along the curb in front of her house putting on lip gloss.

Diana pressed one of the buttons on her car radio and tuned to South Carolina Educational Radio. It was a Monday just after three o'clock and, of course, that meant that Eve's talk show was already in progress. Diana pulled her car out into the slow-moving traffic as the first tiny drops of rain showered her car.

A squeaky little voice issued from the radio. "Hi, Dr. Hayes, this is Sarah."

"Hello, Sarah, and how are you today?" Diana heard Eve say.

"Oh, Dr. Hayes, I'm so sad, so sad and blue. I can't believe this is your last show. Why? Why are you quitting?"

"I'm sorry, Sarah, but it's time for me to move on. I don't want you to feel sad about it. Change is a good thing, and we need to embrace it as part of life."

"But I'm going to miss you. You're like my mentor, and because of you I've realized I don't need a relationship. I'll never get hurt again from chasing after emotional handicaps."

"Emotional handicaps?" Eve said.

"Yes, chasing after love and how that handicaps us as women."

"Sarah, let's not be so nihilistic about love. 'Emotional handicap' is a heavy-handed way to portray love."

"But you were the one who told me that, Dr. Hayes."

Eve took a few seconds to reply, and the dead air stood out as if it were a loud sound. The silence was soon broken by Eve sounding self-assured and strong.

"Sarah, let me say to you and all of my listeners, I was wrong. I was wrong to dispense advice about love and romance, two things I knew very little about until just recently. I was wrong to tell you that searching for love would emotionally handicap you. I am in love and I was wrong."

"But Dr. Hayes, what about your books? What about your research?"

"For my parents, romance had little meaning, and their marriage was a partnership of shared resources and assets. Love became a foreign language to me, and instead of confronting my fears, I convinced myself all successful relationships must be like theirs, but I was wrong. Most successful relationships are loving and passionate."

"Dr. Hayes, I don't know what to say, I just feel—"

Eve interrupted her. "Sarah. Go out, search for your special someone, and don't be afraid to let your guard down. Yes, we may get hurt along the way, but when you find it, and you will, it's a beautiful thing. It will complete you. Sarah, and to all of my other listeners, with this I must say good-bye. I am in love."

Eve said nothing else. There was no sound, and the empty space hung until someone at the station dropped in a promo for an upcoming show. Eve had given her last radio show and confirmed to all that she was in love.

There was a smile on Diana's face as she listened to Eve's final broadcast. Indeed, a sense of accomplishment and relief swelled up inside her. With Eve's last words, "I am in love," Diana said to herself, "Finally."

She could still picture Eve as that quiet young girl she'd met in college. Though sharp of mind and bold intellectually, she was awkward around boys. At first Diana thought she was tragically shy, but during that first summer at Folly, she realized it was much, much more. Her relationship with Porter carried her into adulthood without her having to face her fears. A little romance and passion makes a woman feel alive and beautiful, she thought, and she was so happy that her friend was feeling these things for the first time in her life.

As much as Eve had led a Spartan existence, Diana led the life of an epicure. She had a passion for all things from fine foods and hotels to art and music. Diana lived to love, loved to live, and was a particularly warm and loving mother and wife, despite her infidelities. Defying logic and morals, she believed that if she loved her husband so much, and so strongly, then how bad could an occasional tryst be?

After Jack and the kids arrived in Charleston to the new house, he found sketches she had made of the children while they were gone. He thought they were wonderfully done and told her so, encouraging her to enroll in an art class. It was an evening class at the College of Charleston called "the Human Figure." Once a week at four o'clock she and eight other students worked with acrylics, painting studies of the human form. The past few classes had been about hands and facial features, but tonight they were to do a nude study. The hedonistic side of Diana hoped there would be a male model, and she would not be disappointed.

As soon as she made the turn onto Calhoun Street the storm clouds ripped open and poured down a rain so hard, visibility was a little more than a white blur of water and oncoming headlights. Given that the city parking garage was two blocks away, she circled the block and eventually found a place on the street near the entrance to the art school.

She waited in the car hoping the rain would stop, but as with such things, it came down more heavily than ever. When four o'clock rolled around she made the decision to run for it, and by the time she made the vestibule of the Halsey Institute of Art she was soaked down to her skin. Her hair was dripping wet and the outline of her pale pink bra showed through her white cotton blouse.

Except for the sound of the rain pelting the old building, the art college was quiet. It was late in the afternoon and the studios and classrooms were dark, save for studio G at the end of the hallway. A pool of incandescent light spilled from the open doorway, bathing her in its warm amber radiance as she entered the studio. The smell of paints and turpentine greeted her nose and the colors of many paintings laid out to dry greeted her eyes.

Professor Johnston was sitting on an old metal stool with the strap of his briefcase slung over his shoulder. He was a card-carrying artist who championed the counterculture, looking like a long-haired soldier wearing olive drab army pants and a military-style khaki shirt. Diana saw him look at his watch when she came into the room.

"Ms. Parks, there you are."

"Just barely. That's a hell of a storm."

"I know, I think it's kept the other students away. Another five minutes and I was going to cancel class."

"I'm glad I made it. I was looking forward to the class tonight," she said.

"I'm still considering canceling, since there's just one student. I just texted my partner about an early dinner."

"Oh, please don't cancel."

"Tell you what," he said, "the model gets paid whether we have class or not. If you want to stay and do the nude study you can, but I'm going to leave after you get set up."

"Yes," Diana said without hesitation.

"Okay, but class is officially canceled, and we'll have to do a makeup class for the other students next week. Just consider this your own private session. Go ahead and set up and I'll get the model."

By the time the model walked out of the changing room, Diana had set up her easel and a blank canvas to the right of the raised platform. The wooden TV tray that served as her paint stand was to her left, and atop the stand rested her art box filled with brushes, palette knives, and tubes of paints.

Diana readied her art box and organized her brushes. She was checking which tubes still contained paint until she heard the model stepping up onto the platform. He was as she had hoped he would be. The tall young man, probably twenty years old, was wearing only a white terry bathrobe. His closely cropped dark hair made him look like a Roman centurion, and he had pale-blue eyes made even paler against his olive complexion.

"Ms. Parks, this is Mark Levine. Mark, Ms. Parks."

"Pleased to meet you," Diana said.

"It's my pleasure," he said in a quiet voice.

Diana considered replying, "No, the pleasure is all mine," but thought better of it.

"Okay, I'm out of here," said Professor Johnston. "You have until six o'clock. Just make sure the lights are all off and you lock the door behind you."

After the professor left, Diana grabbed her sketchpad and pencils and approached the model. She walked around him to get a better look.

She readied herself. There was a long moment of silence like the measure in between when the members of an orchestra all play an "A" and that moment before the conductor begins the first wave of his hand. The only sound was the low drum of rain on the roof.

"Let me know when you want the bathrobe off," he said. "I usually wait until people have an idea of a particular pose they want."

"I know what I want," Diana said.

"Okay," he said.

He unbelted his bathrobe with little modesty, turned, and tossed it on an old chair behind him. With his back to her, she saw his small, taut derriere, which looked as if it had been chiseled out of marble. It was when he straightened his body that she saw him in his full statuesque glory. This young man obviously took care of his body: he was not overly muscular, but he had the body of an Olympic swimmer. His legs were taut and muscular from thigh to calf. Given that there was bright and direct light on Mark, he was one of most physically fit men she had ever seen so close. He was magnificent, Magnificent Mark.

"How do you want me to stand?" he asked.

"Just a second."

She walked over to the side, picked up a wooden crate, and placed it on the stage in front of him.

"Here, place your right foot on the crate and place your hands on your hips."

"Like this?"

"Yes. Is that comfortable?"

"Yeah, that's okay."

She took a few steps backward and started sketching a rough outline of Magnificent Mark.

"So, you've done this before?"

"Yes, it's good money, being a student and all. I've been getting a lot of callbacks too."

"So, what are you studying?"

"I'm in the business and marketing program."

"Oh really. As handsome as you are, you could also be a model."

He blushed, even though he had heard that same compliment over a hundred times. "Thank you."

Diana walked back to her easel. She could feel those little areas just below her eyes grow sore, the areas that tightened when she smiled. Her face was locked into a smile she tried to hide, but she gave up trying. She watched him look at her as she took the tubes of paint in her hand and squeezed various colors onto her palette. With a large brush in hand she walked over to him, closer than she had been while she was sketching.

"Now I'm going to mix a little color and try to match your skin tone for the canvas."

Diana dragged a little titanium white into burnt sienna, and added a touch of Naples yellow.

"Not quite right," she said.

She mixed a little more white paint, covered the tip of her brush, and held it about an inch over his arched right thigh near his knee. From over the arch of his thigh, she noticed he was no longer flaccid, there was a growing firmness, and she could see his body slowly flush with color as she touched his knee with her paintbrush.

The drum of the rain increased and she could hear the sound of the wind driving the rain sideways against the window.

Diana moved her brush along his thigh to his buttocks and she could hear his breathing speed up and grow deeper. She moved forward and painted a line along his thigh and back to his knee. She dabbed on more paint and ran the brush along the inside of his thigh, stopping short of his crotch. He was aroused, and so was she. She took a little white and painted a line down his chest and across his stomach to the top of his lower hairline. He was doing his best to keep his pose, but this white line of paint broke his concentration and he reached out for her shoulder. Diana let the palette tumble to the floor and grabbed him, kissing him just below his stomach while he softly caressed her hair. The smell of musk and paint tickled her nose and she watched him swell with excitement from her tender kisses and the touch of her soft hands.

Diana felt his hands slip under her arms as he pulled her up close to him. Now her face was to his and she kissed him on the lips. It was a deep and passionate kiss, his arms wrapping around her as he slipped his hands under her white blouse. His eyes caught hers and he stared at her as he slipped off her blouse and removed her pale pink bra, still damp from the rain. A smile lit up his face as he pulled her close to him, kissing from her breast down to her stomach. He unfastened her jeans, unzipped them, and slowly slipped them and her underwear down to her ankles.

Reaching up, he grabbed her hands and guided her down to the floor. They sat and kissed for a very long time before he touched her body. For most women, a man who takes his time shows a certain tenderness, but for Diana it felt like a tease. She wanted him to squeeze her breast, and she wanted his hand between her legs. With her heart racing, she grabbed his strong hands and slid them over her chest. He looked at her as if she were the only woman in the world and began massaging her breast with a warm firmness.

Her whole body ached for Magnificent Mark and

she wanted him on top of her and the weight of his body bearing down between her legs. She watched his chest heave as he laid her down and rocked into her. It was just the right spot. The slow and steady movement sent shots of sensation over her body until she tensed up. The rhythm increased and she moved her hips forward with his downstrokes. All she could see was his broad chest moving in time with a pace that began to increase until her tense body reached the point where she wanted to be. In a shivering instant, it was all over, and she, like him, collapsed to the floor.

Though her blank canvas still sat on its easel, she had finished her nude study of Mark. Diana was quite satisfied with the results and thought the proportions perfect, the lines harmonious, and the colors deeply shaded. Her artistry had captured the essence of youth and, since she had taken all that the class could offer, there was nothing left for her to learn about the human figure. She never returned to class.

The excitement was long-lasting and for several days the rush of endorphins lingered and intoxicated her every thought. She felt desired, sexy, and every bit in control of her life. It was the sensation she loved the most, and while she had none of the bad habits of the many women she knew who drank too much or popped prescription pills, she was addicted to the act of love. Diana's thoughts were always flooded with images of passionate acts. It was who she was.

On the following Saturday Diana still felt the body rushes and high of desire she had captured in the art studio. She and Jack decided to walk from their home on Rainbow Row to Café Ninety-Nine before her performance. For the first time in nearly twenty years, she would take the stage again for a solo acoustic show of vamped-up country classics and Crazy Hearts favorites.

It was a comfortable stroll through the heart of the historic district. The heat of the July day, blown off by a calm easterly gale, left the brackish scent of salt in the air. The lingering seaborne atmosphere added another layer of smells across the old city.

The place was relatively new to the Charleston scene, and while the previous occupant had been a true restaurant in every sense of the word, Café Ninety-Nine was more of a bar, with a generous outdoor patio and an appetizer menu. Catering more to tourists by day, with quick service and overpriced bar food, during the evening the outdoor space became a popular venue for the local acoustic scene.

While it appeared as a proper patio now, the space had once been the parking lot of the aforementioned restaurant. As such it was just a few steps from the sidewalk of Charleston's Old Market and had a "sunken" feel, with the backside lined with three long steps that rose up to the front walkway of the building. By happenstance, this elevated sidewalk served as a perfect stage. It was just high enough that every seat had a good view.

Black metal mesh tables and matching chairs covered the patio, leaving just enough space for the waitstaff to serve food by day and drinks by night. Surrounding the patio was a short wall punctuated by columns mounted with gaslights, and the spaces in between served as additional seating when unlucky patrons arrived too late to get a table. Tonight was one of those nights, and people lined the outside walls and filled every opening.

Local patrons eager to hear a singer who was one of Charleston's musical legends filled all the available tables. While Diana was not originally from Charleston and her music career had been short-lived, most believed she was a native Charlestonian and they considered Crazy Hearts one of the city's great musical contributions. Many had never seen her, or were too young to have been around when her band was breaking into the national music scene, but her return to the stage had become a must-see event for the Charleston party crowd.

An outsider would have therefore thought it peculiar when Diana, closely followed by Jack and her guitar case, slipped in through the side gate and walked through the crowd, and no one recognized her. Not only do Charlestonians place a greater importance on being seen than on what they see, but the crowd was too wrapped up in drinking down a dozen different conversations to recognize the musical legend they had been told about. Out of this caterwaul, Diana heard a familiar but excited voice.

"Diana," Eve said. "Over here."

To the right, in front of the steps, was a table taken by Lucy, Eve, and Gio. Lucy sat next to an empty chair, wrapped in a Lilly Pulitzer summer dress in a watercolor print of oversized pink camellia flowers on a sea-green background. While the print was bright and youthful, the tailoring free and flowing, on Lucy the dress looked matronly. It was nothing different from what Diana would have expected her to wear. However, Eve surprised her in both her clothing and her attitude. She looked more like a coed than a professor in her Daisy Duke shorts and white T-shirt emblazoned with a large Italian flag and the words "Giovanni's Pasticceria," which proudly flew over her bust line. Eve's blond hair fell on her shoulders and she had curves where none had before existed. Next to her sat Gio, and he was bigger and swarthier than Eve had described him. His dark hair and olive face stood out in contrast to the wrinkled white cotton oxford he was wearing, while an expanse of dark chest hair spread down from between the two unbuttoned edges of his shirt.

Eve jumped out of her seat, squeezing between Gio and the person sitting behind him. She made a mad dash to Diana, almost knocking her over with a linebacker hug, and she gave Jack the same staggering embrace.

"Can you believe this crowd?" Eve said. "We got here at four o'clock and people were already here."

"Amazing, isn't it?" Jack said. "It shows that these people have great taste in music."

Jack's big grin beamed out to Diana, and she smiled back and gave him a kiss.

"It's because you, my dear," Diana said, "are an expert in marketing and PR." She kissed him again. "I don't know what I'd do without him," she said.

Eve *awwed* and looked at both of them lovingly.

"Come over here, you two," Eve said.

She took Diana by the hand and led her to their table.

"Diana, I want you to meet Gio."

Gio jumped to his feet and kissed Diana on one cheek and then the other.

"*Bella donna.* My pleasure," he said. "And you must

be husband."

"Yes. Jack Parks. Nice to meet you."

Jack flinched from Gio's handshake. His massive baker's hand covered Jack's with a solid grasp.

"Much pleasure to meet you too," Gio said.

Lucy, still seated, chose not to rise when Jack stepped over to her. Minor intoxication and a hazy glow had spread over her eyes, induced by that extra glass of wine. A slightly amused smile caused her to look friendly and warm.

"And you must be Lucy," Jack said. "I've heard so much about you."

"Hopefully only the shiny happy things," Lucy said.

She held out her hand in such a way that Jack was unsure if she meant for him to kiss it or shake it. He chose the latter and she shook his hand in a ladylike manner.

"We saved you a seat," Lucy said, "I hope you can watch the show with us."

"Oh yeah. Thanks for thinking of me," he said.

"Great, and you can tell me about how you were able to convince this talented woman to be your wife. She's something special."

"Thank you, Lucy. That's so kind," Diana said.

"Feel the love, y'all," Eve said. "Feel the love."

In the area designated as the stage, a simple wooden barstool sat atop a small cinnabar-colored Persian carpet. There Diana sat while tuning her guitar. In a quiet homage to Johnny Cash, she was wearing all black. A tank top topped Diana's tight black jeans. Her hair fell forward so that it caressed the sides of her face when she tilted her head to look down at her guitar.

When she was satisfied with the sound of her guitar, she reached for the microphone that extended toward her like an outstretched arm from the boom stand, and tapped it. She followed the thump, thump, thump of her taps with the ubiquitous, "Check, check, check," and after a strum of her guitar she got a thumbs-up from Jack, who was sitting next to Lucy in the front row.

It had been a long time since she had performed, but Diana seemed as comfortable sitting in front of the crowd as she would have been sitting in her own living room talking with friends. The audience reacted in the same intimate way and all the bar talk and background conversations began to fade away as she readied herself.

"Hello, I'm Diana Villiers," she said.

She often used her maiden name when it suited her. During the short pause while the audience came to order, she strummed her guitar and adjusted the tuning on her high E string a little more.

"Some of y'all might remember the band I started right here in Charleston."

A few of the older members of the audience began to clap and cheer, causing Diana to smile.

"We were called the Crazy Hearts and we had a couple of songs on the radio, oh, about twenty years ago."

There were a couple of shouts from the audience and someone cheered, while a few others applauded.

"I want to thank y'all for coming out tonight, and Café Ninety-Nine for letting me play. It feels good to be back where it all started, here in Charleston, the greatest city in the world."

Charlestonians love being complimented, and

Diana's praise of the old city garnered more applause, some from people who had no clue as to what kind of music Diana was going to play.

After she had slipped on her thumb pick, Diana lightly strummed her guitar and pulled the microphone closer to her mouth.

"Tonight I'm going to perform some of those Crazy Hearts tunes, but first I want to do a few of my favorite country classics, including the very first song I ever learned. It's a song that's really about two very different women. The first a woman who has what it takes to get what she wants, and the second a woman who pleads with the first to stay away from her man. Now, ladies, I don't know about y'all, but I'd rather be the first woman."

A few women laughed and there was a huge grin on her face. It was not so much because of her joke, but because she saw Gio pouring the last of a pitcher of Long Island iced tea into Eve's glass. She watched Eve heartily drink it down, and when the women made eye contact Eve smiled back while wiping her lips with the back of her hand.

"Seriously, though, it's a beseechingly beautiful song, by one of the greatest performers out there, Miss Dolly Parton. I'm talking about 'Jolene,' and it's the first song I ever learned. In fact, there are two women in the audience tonight, two of my best friends from college. They were there early on in my journey as a musician. It was our first summer together, and when I learned this song, I discovered the musician in me. Thanks to them, it's the reason I'm here tonight."

Diana strummed an A chord and grinned at Eve and Lucy.

She launched into the syncopated guitar riff from Parton's original, but she sang in the raw style that had been her trademark sound when she fronted Crazy Hearts. She belted out "Jolene, Jolene, Jolene, Jolene" like a one-two-three-four punch, then followed the song with a Texas swing version of Hank Williams's "Settin' the Woods on Fire." The audience clapped along, and Diana's energetic delivery revved them up. They wanted more and Diana gave it to them with her own version of "Folsom Prison Blues," which was faster and grungier than Cash's mournful version.

Slowing things down, Diana played Chris Isaak's soft-voiced version of Marty Robbins's classic "Return to Me." She demonstrated her ability to play finger-style on guitar. The crowd grew silent as she played a Spanish-inspired guitar solo. It was as if the whole city had fallen into a hush to hear her fingers flicker along the dark-brown wood grain of the guitar neck. The quiet was still there after the last note, broken by a gust of wind that introduced the applause from the audience.

She had hit her stride, and when the applause of the audience faded, she began playing acoustic versions of her band's songs. The first song she played was "Pleasure Bound." The tune was originally a rocked out anthem to the needs of women, but tonight, she sang it differently.

Strumming the guitar hard, Diana played with a bouncy rhythm that was more reminiscent of the folk-pop of the Beatles. It sounded bright and fresh instead of the declarations of an angst filled young woman.

Was never one to give apologies
And you'll never hear a regret from me
Never been captive of conformity
Sometimes on the verge of insanity

It's the way I live and the way I love
It's a wanton way of a lonesome dove
It's a choice I make as the world goes round
It's a lovely road when you're pleasure bound

Like a tiger I'll never change my stripes
I will never give up without a fight
It's the captive heart that's bound to let slip
From a warm embrace and a lover's lips

It's the way I live and the way I love
It's a wanton way of a lonesome dove
It's a choice I make as the world goes round
It's a lovely road when you're pleasure bound

What a woman wants is a woman's needs
A whole lot of love is what I believe
It's from this passion that I feel the urge
To set my heart free so my soul will surge

It's the way I live and the way I love
It's a wanton way of a lonesome dove
It's a choice I make as the world goes round
It's a lovely road when you're pleasure bound

After the first two verses Diana played a folksy riff
that inspired the audience to clap along with the beat
before she played a bridge and doubled the chorus
with a "la-la-la-la-la-a-la-la-la-la."

She gave new life to "First Blush" by slowing down the tempo and turning it into a ballad. Picking up the pace, she performed rocked-up versions of "Chase the Sun" and "Black-Winged Angel."

She grinned as she sang the chorus.

> I may be a black-winged angel
> with a tarnished halo
> But I've never been one to be
> all surface and shallow
> I've got my own wings and it's my
> destiny I'll follow
> I'm just a black-winged angel
> with a tarnished halo

Song after song, she played the history of her life as translated by the music she and the band had written, played, and lived. The excitement of performing coursed through her body, and this night on the stage was more satisfying than anything she could remember. It was who she'd once been and it satisfied an empty space that until now she'd had no understanding of how to fill.

"Thank you, thank you," she said, "ya'll are too kind. I've got one more song to play tonight. It's a new one I just wrote."

Diana took a moment to make sure her guitar was in tune.

"This next song is a little different for me. It's actually a waltz for guitar. I want to dedicate it to my two friends Lucy and Eve."

Diana nodded at them and began to count, "one-two-three, one-two-three, one-two-three."

When I was young and unknowing,
like the snow on a mountainside,
Your warmth caused my un-thawing,
like sun warming the valley wide,
And I came down from the mountain,
like a river through the divide.

And all at once we danced the dance,
like wisps of smoke in the four winds,
And now that time has passed us by,
and I need you now my dear friends,
Will you still go waltzing with me,
dancing until the music ends?

Our friendships came without warning,
and we shared the joys and the tears,
To the winds and moon melodies,
and after the cloudy day clears,
We found a beautiful passage,
and our friendships we held so dear.

And all at once we danced the dance,
like wisps of smoke in the four winds,
And now that time has passed us by,
and I need you now my dear friends,
Will you still go waltzing with me,
dancing until the music ends?

Now I am older and knowing,
I'm worn of the way I have been,
I just can't go any further,
I know my spirit needs to mend,
And when I realize what was real,
it was always with my dear friends.

And all at once we danced the dance,
like wisps of smoke in the four winds,
And now that time has passed us by,
and I need you now my dear friends,
Will you still go waltzing with me,
dancing until the music ends?

She had performed the song with a side-to-side sway, and the audience followed her motions as she strummed her guitar with a one-two-three rhythm. The audience was a dancing wave, and as she finished she punched out the last chords, standing up and holding her guitar out. The audience followed suit and stood up too when they gave their applause. Eve, Gio, Jack, and even Lucy were on their feet as Diana took a bow. Her first night performing in so many years had been a resounding success, and she was excited about performing the next night.

Inspired by the success of the show, Diana was determined to reinvent herself as the musician she'd once been. Even before she finished her last song, she had made up her mind to hand off her business duties to Jack and their new manager. The feeling that came over her was nostalgic.

In college she'd discovered she was a natural musician, and performing had helped her weather her parents' divorce and the loss of support from her mother afterward. Her mother had said she'd never make it in the music business—the same mother who had sunk everything she owned, including her marriage, to launch the career of her then-boyfriend Ricky Ray Tyler. Jack had told Diana her mother was wrong, and that if she really wanted something, if she had faith in herself as a musician, she could do anything. As the faith grew in her heart, she had become able to express herself through music.

There always seemed be an empty space inside her, a place that was passionate and sensual, and tonight she'd filled this empty place with the intimacy a performer gives to an audience when she bares her soul. Over the years that loss of playing and performing had caused Diana to slip into dark places. While she had no regrets, there were things she had done, such as her infidelity at the art studio, that seemed so far away now and committed by someone else. Tonight there was a feeling of warmth inside her, a need for more meaning in her life. Diana realized that the meaning she sought was in making a true commitment to Jack as a wife and friend, in being a better mother to her children, and in liberating her sensual side by performing again.

WALTZING in VIENNA

~12~

PARIS

Despite living in a huge house and having collections of fine wines and antiques, Lucy owned only one thing that she considered extravagant and indulgent. Eight years ago, when she and Theo went to Paris to close on their apartment, they'd visited the Louis Vuitton store on the Champs-Élysées. Lucy, so taken by the luxury and exclusivity of the luggage, stood in the store grinning and examining everything. She almost cried when they had to leave. Just as they were about to flag a taxi back to their hotel, Theo took her back into the store and offered to buy a set of luggage for her, and she accepted. Before returning home she packed their clothes in the new suitcase and abandoned their old luggage at the hotel. The suitcase and two matching bags were in pristine condition, not because they were well taken care of, which they were, but because the bags had come out of storage only once when Hilton had presented Theodore with a Spirit of Pride Award in Beverly Hills five years ago.

She packed her prettiest things. There were two new summer dresses in canary and indigo, and a green linen afternoon dress with three-quarter-length sleeves, a faux shawl collar, and a gilded griffin belt buckle. She packed her best lingerie, beautiful things in pink, red, and black. On a lark she packed the garter she'd worn on her wedding day. The smaller bag contained two pairs of flats and three pairs of pumps in various colors. The final item she packed was her vintage-inspired short-sleeved dress in black with pink roses. The belted dress was very flattering and enhanced her full figure. It was Theodore's favorite and she knew his preference for her curves. While many men gawk at the models in their wives' copies of the Victoria's Secret catalog, Lucy would often watch Theodore leafing through her latest Lane Bryant catalog.

It was not long after she telephoned the taxi service that the car arrived. The driver tapped his horn and shifted his car along the curb in front of the old wrought iron gate. Lucy was already on the front porch with her bags. For the long trip, she'd chosen a comfortable black warm-up suit with green trim and coordinating tennis shoes. The chocolate-colored Louis Vuitton handbag suspended from her left shoulder added to her casual chic.

Lucy followed the driver to the car as he took her bags and loaded them into the trunk. It was empowering. She had arranged everything herself, made the reservations, and purchased the tickets. International travel on her own initiative thrilled her, and once she was in the taxi, she double-checked her passport and papers. Her life was in motion and not stuck in some kind of holding pattern.

Charleston International Airport serves as a regional hub, and checking her luggage and getting her boarding pass was surprisingly easy. At the gate the airline offered her a first-class upgrade for the entire trip and she took the offer and delighted in boarding with her Louis Vuitton handbag and slipping into seat 1D in the first-class section of the plane. Next to her in seat 1C was a young woman on her way to a senate internship in Washington, DC. She was a plump brunette named Anna, smartly dressed in a navy skirt and pale-yellow blouse. Her youthful glow and excitement reminded Lucy of herself when she was in college. While comparing herself to younger women sometimes made her think of what could have been, today it caused her to believe in what could be.

Anna had earned a degree in business at the Darla Moore School of Business at USC. She passionately spoke about new legislation on tax reform, tax code disadvantages for US businesses, and the growing issue of large inversion deals by US corporations. Impressed by this young woman, Lucy expressed her own concerns about property taxes. She also complimented Anna on her shoes. When Anna boarded the plane, Lucy had admired her navy high heels. She knew they were expensive because of the perfectly defined tip of the shoe and the luster of the blue leather, and when Anna slipped one off, Lucy saw the Jimmy Choo label. Their conversation about taxes and shoes ended when they landed at the Charlotte airport. The time had flown by, but in a beautiful and relaxing way.

Lucy had a three-hour layover before she was to

connect with her international flight, and rather than take a chance on what the airline might serve, she looked at the layover as an opportunity to have an early dinner at the airport food court. She also decided to order something she had never eaten before, a lamb gyro and fries.

While eating, Lucy sent text messages to Eve about how excited she was to be going on her little adventure to surprise Theo. Eve was happy for her old friend, and she let her know that one is never too old to fall in love again. Instead of the grammatically correct text messages she had always received from Eve, Lucy smiled at Eve's texts filled with emoticons and abbreviations she did not understand. Eve sent text after text about the love she was feeling for Gio, and even sent her a picture of the chicken cacciatore he was making her for dinner.

Their texts ended with a phone call from Theodore at four o'clock Lucy's time. He was about to go to bed and was calling to ask if Teddy and William had made the cut for the Citadel honor guard. Lucy was concerned he might hear the background noise of the airport and figure out her surprise, but he did not notice. He was pleased once she told him both boys had made the honor guard, and he told her it had been a long day and he was ready to go to bed. Theodore said he missed her and wished he were home with her, and told her good night.

The flight was on time, and at five thirty Lucy boarded the Paris-bound plane and prepared for the nearly eight-hour flight. She slept most of the way, and because of the time change, she arrived at Charles de Gaulle Airport just before seven a.m. the next day.

The pilot had given gate information and the weather forecast as they made their approach over the Paris skyline. The next week promised to be beautiful, with highs in the mideighties, warm for Parisians, but more than comfortable for a Charlestonian. The flight had been perfect, and while it had been long and tiring for most of the passengers, Lucy felt revitalized as the wheels touched down on the landing strip.

Beneath the grand elliptical domed ceiling, the crowd at the airport buzzed with activity. The dome seemed like a hive to Lucy, and the people all bees. Some ran and some walked, departing the airport for myriad reasons, from business meetings to reunions with family and friends. Some were obviously tourist carrying their purchases from the duty-free shop. The airport was very much alive.

It was an overpowering sensation to be in a man-made hive built for itinerant occupants. The international terminal was awash with languages from all over Europe and beyond. Her confidence was building as she asked for directions: all at once her French came back to her. She retrieved her bags and made her way to the French customs counter with little delay.

With one bag over her shoulder and the other mounted on the rolling suitcase behind her, she looked for a restroom, and found one near the exit to the taxi lane. Lucy went into one of the brightly colored stalls, removed her travel clothes, and slipped into the black dress with pink roses. She switched her tennis shoes out for pantyhose and black pumps, and packed her traveling clothes into her suitcase.

Emerging from the airport, she slipped on her sunglasses and looked every bit the fashionable

Parisian woman as she hailed a Taxi Parisian to take her to the apartment.

The driver's name was Amir. He knew she was an American, but complimented her French with his own version of the language, seasoned by his thick Turkish accent. They made small talk. He told her about his newborn son back home, and how much he wished that his baby and wife could be in Paris with him. In turn she told him that she was in Paris to surprise her husband. Amir said her husband was a lucky man to have a woman who would travel so far to see him.

Amir's taxi wove through the congested fabric in the heart of the city and down the busy stretch of the Champs-Élysées to the eighth district. The car turned and headed up Rue Arsene Houssaye, revealing a bone-white six-story building with wrought iron Juliet balconies.

"Stop here, *arrêtez-vous ici*," Lucy said.

The taxi came to rest at the street corner in front of Liébaus Chocolatier, one of the businesses that occupied the ground level of the apartment building.

"*Madame, s'il vous plaît,*" he said, "*cinquante-trois euros.*"

Lucy hesitated and tried to remember.

"Feeftay-tree, in Anglish. *Oui?*" he said.

"*Oui. Bien sûr,*" she said.

She paid him and he unloaded her luggage at the foot of the doorway to the building's lobby. She rolled her bags across the old parquet floor and rode the elevator up to the fifth floor. The elevator made her appreciate having paid the extra premium for the apartment.

When the elevator door opened, she turned down

the long hallway. It was well lit and the molding and carpet very French and cheerful. The smell of someone's breakfast, coffee and fresh toast, spilled from one of the nearby apartments. She could hear the sounds of people getting ready for the new day, muffled conversations and the sound of a French news show on someone's television.

At the end of the hallway was apartment 5G, and she fished a little silver key from the outside pocket of her handbag. The never-used key turned stiffly, but with a good twist, she opened the door and entered a small living area. The furnishings looked different from what she remembered from first decorating the apartment. They looked newer and softer, but she thought it was her memory that had turned soft.

Down the hallway she saw the door to the bathroom. Light seeped out from under the bottom of the door and she could see the lines of a shadow moving about. There was the sound of running water, and when it stopped, the door opened and Theodore was standing there. His hair was wet and he had a towel wrapped around his waist. A cloud of warm air bellowed out, thick with the smell of a shower and of soap. Theodore saw her, but he stopped dead in the doorway. He was frozen in place; even the breath that he had been about to take stopped. His face was emotionless, flat, and his cheeks flushed. It was not the reaction she had hoped for.

"Surprise," Lucy said.

Her first thought was that he must be sick, maybe that he'd had a heart attack, because of the look of shock in his eyes. Her second thought was that something was wrong about her being there. She quickly realized her presence was unwelcome.

"What are you doing here?" Theodore asked.

The tone of his voice was not joyous and he was not happy to see her, nor was there any expression of surprise in his eyes, only a look of shock that was turning to anger.

"I came to surprise you. Our anniversary is coming up."

"You should have called."

His eyes darted to the open door to the bedroom on his right.

"Why?" she asked.

She began to walk down the hall to the bedroom, but Theodore took a long step forward and blocked her from entering.

"Let's go talk in the living room," he said.

"No. I'm going into the bedroom."

Before Lucy took another step, she saw a shadow in the darkened bedroom move forward and walk through the door. It was a woman. She was young, probably in her midtwenties. Her medium-length blond hair was tousled and she was wearing one of Theodore's white T-shirts, which looked huge over her very petite frame. She was not even his type and the exact opposite of Lucy.

"Theo, *ce qui se passe?*" the woman said, "*Qui est-ce?*"

"*Il n'y à personne,*" he said, "*Retourne au lit.*"

"I'm nobody?" Lucy said. "But I'm your wife."

Lucy's heart was pounding. She could feel the rhythm thumping hard inside her, causing her whole body to tremble, while her breathing was rapid and heavy.

"*Retourne au lit,*" he said again.

"Don't you dare tell her to leave," Lucy said.

Lucy stepped in front of the bedroom door and

blocked her.

"*Je suis sa femme,*" Lucy yelled at the woman. "I'm his goddammed wife!"

The woman backed away. "*Vous êtes sa femme?*" she said. "*Non, non, non. Je suis sa femme.*"

The woman put her hand on her heart and said, "Me his wife," and she looked up at Theodore.

"Papa?" a little girl said from the other bedroom.

The door creaked open and a young girl peeked through the opening. The girl was no more than three years old and she was wearing fuzzy pink pajamas.

Lucy backed away and covered her mouth with her hand, scared, and overwhelmed with shock. A sudden wave of queasiness consumed her from the inside and she felt as if she would crumple into a pile of infinite sadness. If she stayed another second, the reality would hit her even harder and destroy her. It would be best, she thought, to run away from it all and hope she would wake up from this dark dream. Perhaps she was in the wrong apartment and this man was not Theo. It must be a mistake, but this was all very real, too real.

When she turned to leave, she tripped over her suitcases, tumbled across the floor, and fell against the door. Theodore did nothing, said nothing, and only stared at Lucy as if she were some kind of stranger. Clutching her purse, she got back on her feet and looked at Theodore one last time. Her senses were overwhelmed. The once-clear visages of Theodore, the woman, and the child were now fuzzy shadows. She tried to speak, but could not form the words, could not make a sound. Without thinking, she flung herself toward the door and out into the now-gloomy hallway, the antithesis of what it had been minutes before. The darkness surrounded her like the murky waters of the River Styx, flowing to the elevator, which must certainly descend to the underworld.

When she stepped out of the dark apartment building, the bright light of the day was muted and gray, and all the colors of the buildings, cars, and people seemed to have been flushed to someplace far away. The streets were unknown to her and the inhabitants unrecognizable. It was not the Paris she'd dreamed of, and she was a stranger in a strange land. It was not the City of Light, nor the City of Love. This Paris frightened her and she fell into an unconscious state of reality rather than a conscious state of shock.

"Carte de crédit, s'il vous plaît," the man said.

Lucy stared blankly at him. He was a slight little man with thin lips tightly pursed into a kind of perturbed pucker. Standing behind the oversized counter, his small frame seemed childlike.

"Your cwedit card, pwease," he said.

There was a lisp in his voice that made it difficult to understand not only his English, but his native French too.

Lucy dug through her purse and passed the shiny silver card to him. He looked over the counter. *"Vous avez des bagages?"* he asked.

"No baggage," Lucy said. *"Demain je vais avoir besoin de la navette pour l'aéroport."*

"Huit heures, s'il vous plaît."

"Eight?" she said.

He nodded his head and said *oui* with his puckered

lips. "Welcome to Hotel Ibis CDG."

Lucy slipped the key card into her purse and walked through the lobby. She passed by the brightly lit restaurant; not having an appetite, she walked into the lounge in the rear. It was just after six o'clock and only a few people were at the bar. Three men sat at the bar drinking beer, while a young couple sat in the squat purple leather chairs on the sidewall of the lounge. The bright lighting made them look picture-perfect, but Lucy had hoped to find a dark corner because she was feeling less than perfect. She asked the bartender for a glass of Cabernet, which she escorted to a table in the darker rear corner of the lounge.

The last nine hours were a blur to her. She remembered walking through Paris's central shopping areas, passing tourists and street cafés, but little else. She had not cried yet. One cries over a broken heart, but this feeling was like being gutted, as if all the air had emptied from her lungs and her heart and body had been drained of all life. It left her feeling dead inside. Tomorrow she would cry.

The one feeling she was aware of was thirst. The wine went down nicely, and she flagged down the barmaid for another glass. After a few more glasses of wine, her senses had slowly dulled, and she was glad of it. The wine helped fade the shock and pain, and the gutted and empty feeling was fading to a dull numb feeling. Wine can be a wonderful thing.

She smiled for a moment, not because anything that had happened today was funny, but because of how ludicrous Theodore had looked standing in the hallway wearing only a towel next to that clueless young girl. She laughed to herself about how very foolish he was to believe that a girl that young actually saw something in him other than his money. He was a very stupid man, she thought, but she quit smiling when she realized she was a very stupid woman not to have realized her marriage had slipped from her grasp a long time ago.

A lone man at the end of the bar drinking beer sent over her next glass of wine. When the barmaid placed the glass on the table, he raised his glass in a toast to Lucy. He was young, college-aged, with blond curly hair and pale-blue eyes. She could see his eyes even better when he approached her table.

"*Sprechen Sie Deutsch?*" he asked.

"No, sorry," she said. "*Parlez-vous français?*"

"*Nein. Português?*" he asked.

"No. English?" Lucy asked.

The man smiled at her and burst out laughing. "*Nein.*"

Lucy had to laugh. There were four languages between them, yet none of them did they have in common. She understood very little, only that he was a music student named Peter from Austria and he played both guitar and piano. He was on his way back home from Brazil and he mostly talked about bossa nova music, thumping out rhythms on the table. The only English he knew was the lyrics to "The Girl from Ipanema," which he quietly sang to Lucy with his best Portuguese accent, sounding very much like Astrud Gilberto.

The only things he understood were her name—he called her "Luzy"—and that she was an American from Charleston, flying back home in the morning. Despite the language barrier, they talked babble for two hours, and in a strange way, it was comforting to

Lucy. She had a handsome young man flirting with her, and as long as she smiled, she could say anything to him and he would find it interesting. She drank her wine and he his beer and both felt the better for it.

The two fell into the elevator, drunk on wine and beer and flirtations. On the way up he tried to kiss her, but Lucy laughed and dodged the kiss. He smiled back at her and sang, "Yes, he would give his heart gladly." Humming the next line until the elevator stopped on his floor, he turned around and sang, "She looks straight ahead—not at he," and before he could step out of the elevator, Lucy pulled him back in and pressed the button again for her floor. When the elevator door closed, she kissed him and he her, until they tumbled into her room on the ninth floor.

She had never cheated on her husband, never considered it, and she had never been promiscuous when she was a girl. Lucy realized this handsome young man wanted her only for sex and that tomorrow he would be gone, but she wanted it too. He was an anonymous man who wanted an anonymous woman, and tonight she felt sexy for the first time in many years. For now at least, this was her cure for the pain, to be someone else, someone desired.

When she awoke, Peter was gone. After a very physical night, the covers and sheets of the bed were as tangled and twisted as her hair. She felt wrecked and her body ached from trying things she had never done before, and instead of feeling sexy and desired as she had last night, she felt dirty and unwanted. If she had had the time she would have fallen into an endless hole of self-pity, but she'd overslept and had to rush out the door, just barely making a late shuttle to the airport. She was worried she would miss her flight, but with only her purse, she was able to make it to the terminal with ten minutes to spare. She immediately boarded the plane and sat in coach at the back.

She tried to sleep during the flight to Charlotte, but instead read and reread the in-flight magazine. The flight was all a blur, and so was the two-hour layover in Charlotte and the short flight to the Charleston airport. None of it seemed real.

When Lucy stepped out of a dull-yellow taxi that had come to a halt in front of her house, she was still wearing the black dress with pink roses. Thirteen hours from Paris to Charleston with little sleep or food had worn her threadbare. She was still in shock, jet-lagged from the time change, and disgusted by her one-night stand. It had all taken its toll. Her brown eyes were bloodshot, and her long and beautiful hair was a disheveled mess. Still, she felt worse than she looked, worse than she had ever felt in her entire life.

An older couple from down the street passed her as she was paying the driver. They were dressed up for their usual Saturday supper with their neighbors down the street. Lucy knew the woman from the Garden Club and she could feel them staring at her. She knew the woman well enough to know that her unbefitting arrival would be the fodder for the next day's gossip at church.

She felt like a stranger as she walked into the house where she'd spent her childhood and raised two sons. The photographs of countless ancestors looked unfamiliar, as did the antique furniture that had been in her family for decades, some of it for over a century. With the boys gone, the house looked unfriendly and uncomfortable. Indeed, the house had never been comfortable. It was a stuffy display of tradition and was only a home because Lucy had made it so.

Lucy stood in the family room and stared at the portrait of the four of them at the beach. She wondered who the smiling woman was between Theodore and her sons. In a silver frame on the corner of the mantel was the small photograph used to make the painting. Her mother had taken the picture one summer day when they were staying with her at the beach. It was not long after she'd given Lucy and Theo the house on the Battery. Her mother had told her she did not want to live in such a big house by herself, and would be more at home living on the beach in a simple cottage. Lucy had always wondered about her decision, and now she had some idea of the reason behind it. She grabbed her keys and headed to Folly Beach.

She had left her house in an exhausted haze and the next thing she knew, she was pulling into the old driveway at the beach house. It had been shuttered and locked up for some time. Skeletal palmetto trees cast their long shadows across the overgrown yard. The salt air and summer sun had caused the paint to peel and with no one living there to maintain it, the house was in very bad shape. Lucy had always felt the old house had a soul, and it was her connection to the Bonneau family, her mother, and Aunt Catherine. The connection was fading like the memory of who she'd once been. The old soul of the house was aching. When she passed by the front porch, she had to step over the fallen sign that read "Maison de la Folie."

Around the yard she walked, stepping over weeds and climbing up the steps to the back deck. Some of her best memories were of this part of the house. When she was little, she'd spent the summer days pretending it was the deck of a pirate ship, and in the evenings she would sit out after dinner with Aunt Catherine and talk about books. She remembered when she was in college and she and her friends would waltz in Vienna. Her last memories of this old deck were also of her mother. It had been a warm June, just before her mother died, when Lucy had driven down with Teddy and William. They were only twelve years old and Theodore had left for a month-long business trip. She could still see the two of them, innocent and sweet, sitting on top of the table eating watermelon. But those days were long gone, and the house was now nothing more than a wooden marker for her memories. She felt dirty, ugly, and unwanted, and she wanted to wash it all away. Lucy walked down the wooden walkway, down to the gray sandy shore.

She stood at the water's edge beneath the long shadow of the house. The sun was setting on the other side. Dark lines of purple and black hung over the beach, in contrast to the golden rays behind her. The horizon over the ocean's edge was turning into a dark void and she began to march toward it, kicking her shoes off and tossing her purse into the water.

Her black-and-pink dress floated in the water, moving with the ebb and flow of the waves as her feet began to sink into the soft sand. The first big wave rolled in and almost knocked her down. When it retreated, it pulled her deeper until the water enveloped her body. There was no more soft sand beneath her feet, she was floating, and she could feel the undertow pulling at her like cold blue hands. Her eyes burned as the salt water lapped her face and the briny taste of the ocean filled her mouth and nostrils.

She was gasping and disoriented, but there was no panic in her eyes, no thrashing about, and no fighting to say afloat. Instead she let herself go, like a leaf on the water. The ocean began to swell, lifting her up and spinning her around in a contorted dance. Her head came around and she looked back at the house one last time, suspended on the top of the wave until it bottomed out. The undertow tugged at her legs, pulling her down, as a large wave rolled over her head, swallowing her into the abyss, and she was gone.

~13~

RETURN TO FOLLY BEACH

"**W**hat time is Eve going to pick you up?" Jack asked.

Diana was putting on a pair of black high heels. She was wearing an A-line black linen skirt and a matching top with half sleeves, and sitting on a chocolate-colored sofa in her living room.

"One o'clock."

"And you still don't know what happened?"

"No," she said, "not really."

Diana stood up and walked around the room.

"God, I hate heels."

"I'm sorry about your friend."

"Me too. I don't know why she would do it. She was a smart woman, and even though she was old-fashioned, she was very pretty. I always wished I had her figure."

"Didn't she live in one of those big houses on the bay?"

"Yes, and she and her husband were well off."

"What about her husband?"

"He came back into town last weekend after someone found her purse and shoes washed up on the shore."

"The poor guy must be devastated."

"Eve said she called him a couple of times, but he didn't want to talk about it."

"I can't imagine. Is there anything we can do for him?"

"Probably not. No one knows where he's staying. Their house is empty, and up for sale."

"But you think the invitation came from him?"

"Yes."

"Can I see it?" Jack asked.

Diana passed the manila-colored card to Jack.

Your Presence Is Requested
to Celebrate the Life and Passing of
Lucille Pendleton
At a Private Ceremony
Three O'Clock on Saturday
Three-Seventy-Three West Atlantic Avenue
Folly Beach, South Carolina

Riverrun, past Eve and Adam's, from swerve of shore to bend of bay, brings us by a commodius vicus of recirculation back to Howth Castle and Environs.

"That last bit is a little odd," he said.

"I looked it up," she said. "It's the opening to *Finnegan's Wake*. It means something about the recirculation of a river through the Garden of Eden."

The sound of a horn being tapped three short times echoed from the street.

"That must be her," Diana said.

Eve was waiting for her along the curb, and when she unlocked the door for Diana, she whispered a somber "Hi."

Diana could tell she had been crying. Her eyes swollen, she blinked rapidly. The two women barely spoke during the short drive to Folly Beach. Without the sound of the radio or conversation, the road noise seemed to grow in volume and the occasional bump when they crossed the bridges sounded with a vociferous thud.

Eve's car shot over the causeway and they passed by the old Piggly Wiggly. The side road, now widened and paved, led to a high-end housing development. While Porgy's Porch was still there, it was no longer a family-operated seafood house, but a gift shop selling towels and beach accessories, with two more locations at Folly Beach and a new location on Kiawah Island.

They soon crossed the bridge flanked by marshes drained of their water by the low tide. Neither Diana nor Eve had been back since their summers in college, and the once-residential beach community had grown into a resort town with condominiums and town homes in every corner. Loggerhead's Beach Grill and the Crab Shack, once casual hangouts, were now sit-down restaurants where reservations were required. It was not the laid-back beach-bum place they remembered from their college days.

From the boardwalk down, high-rise hotels lined the eastern side of West Atlantic Avenue, all of them sharing a sharply eroding beach. Farther down the road were a few family homes here and there, but most of the beachfront lots were crammed with more condominiums.

The Bonneau family house was one of the exceptions. It stood out as one of the last of the original cottages. To its left was the old Taylor house, still as they remembered it, but to the right of Lucy's beach house sat a modern quadruplex.

Someone had cleaned up the yard, mowed the grass, and trimmed the bushes, and all of the yard debris had been picked up and carted away. A fresh coat of mint-green paint made the house stand out, bright and proud, and the storm shutters popped from a fresh coat of shiny black. They were wide open and the clean windows glistened in the sunlight. The screen door had also been painted black, and the front deck washed and stained a honey glaze. To the left of the door hung a rectangular panel with the words "A House of One's Own" painted in dark green on a white background. Pink roses were painted in the corners.

Diana and Eve walked up the steps to the front door and lightly knocked. They waited and heard nothing and knocked again. Upon the second knock they heard the sound of the deadbolt turning and the rustle and twist of the lock on the other side. When the door swung open Lucy stood before them, very much alive and smiling at them. She had a look of devilish satisfaction on her face.

Lucy wore no makeup and had cut off most of her hair, which was tousled and comfortable. She had worn it long her entire life and the new shorter hairstyle suited her heart-shaped face. Her khaki shorts and short-sleeved yellow blouse revealed her soft middle-aged arms and legs. She looked very comfortable, and because she had abandoned her outdated hair and clothing, she looked younger. Her fresh face beamed with a genuine smile.

"Lucy," Eve screamed.

Before she could move or utter a word, Eve grabbed her and gave her a big hug. She was in tears. "Oh my God, we thought you were dead," she said.

"You've got some explaining to do," Diana said. "I can't believe you scared us like that."

Diana, who rarely cried, was in tears, and she too reached out to hug Lucy.

"Theodore told me you drowned," Eve said, "and why is your house in town empty and up for sale? And what's with these wake invitations?"

"Whoa. Wait a minute," Lucy said. "Come on in and I will explain it all."

Eve and Diana followed Lucy into the house. It was very different from what they remembered. The pine cabinets, freshly painted white, had new black pulls, and the old countertops were gone. In their stead were white granite countertops. There were new stainless steel appliances, and the old kitchen sink had been replaced with a new apron sink.

Throughout the house new sheetrock covered the old knotty pine–paneled walls, painted a crisp white. The floors had been replaced too, by shiny honey-finished oak. Three comfortable off-white love seats anchored the center of the room, arranged in a horseshoe pattern around a simple but sturdy oak coffee table. In the back corner, two larger bookshelves filled with books had replaced the old overburdened bookshelf. Next to this, facing the window overlooking the back deck, sat a sturdy writing table. Atop the shiny desk sat a laptop with a printer neatly resting to its left. A stack of paper in a black plastic tray sat at the top right corner.

There was very little else in this expansive space, and the only items that remained from the old house were the dozens of family pictures that lined the right wall.

"Come and have a seat," Lucy said.

Lucy was grinning. Resting on the coffee table was a bottle of wine, three glasses, and a small silver box. Lucy picked up the bottle and a corkscrew.

"This is a 1971 Château Lafite Rothschild," Lucy said, "the year of my birth. I found it at the house in town when I cleared out the wine cellar. There was a piece of tape with my name written on it. Even from beyond, my mother left me a little gift."

"So, what the hell happened, Lucy?" Diana said.

"And why didn't you return my phone calls?" Eve said.

"I know I should have called," she said, "but it's taken me a little time to sort out what was next for me."

"We thought you were dead," Eve said, "and Theodore, he was so despondent and couldn't tell me very much. All he said was a beachcomber found your purse and shoes floating in the surf. When I called the Folly Beach police they told me they were investigating a break-in here."

"Theo can go fuck himself," Lucy said, "all the way back to Paris."

Lucy's blunt reply caught Diana and Eve off guard. "What?" Diana said.

"The only reason he was despondent, as you say, was because I canceled all of his credit cards. My purse? He learned about that when he called his sister to beg her to wire money to him so he could fly home from Paris."

Lucy opened the bottle of wine with care. She caressed the bottle and poured three glasses, passing two to Diana and Eve. She held her glass up for a toast.

"Tchin-tchin," she said.

The others replied, "Tchin-tchin," and they clinked their glasses.

"Should I begin before or after I discovered Theodore had another wife in Paris? With, I might add, a daughter, and living in our apartment. Turns out Theodore's long business trips were excuses for him to spend more time with his French tart. She's twenty-five at most. The Hilton St. Germain? Another lie, that hotel was finished last year."

Lucy tipped her wineglass and inhaled deeply.

"*In vino veritas*. In wine there is truth. Do you know who said that?" Lucy paused for a moment and replied to her own question, "Plato."

She sipped her wine.

"God, that's terrible, Lucy," Diana said. "When did you get home?"

"I flew to Paris. Of course, you already know that, to surprise him for our anniversary. And boy did I surprise him...and me. I felt gutted. He ripped my heart out. I wandered the streets for hours before deciding to fly back home the next day."

"Lucy," Eve said, "my heart aches so much to hear that. Why didn't you call me?"

"When I got home, I realized my life, the house in town, and the facade with Theodore was nothing more than a walking shadow of a marriage. Even my mother had been more of herself than I had become. I thought about her and this old house and immediately drove down here."

Lucy poured herself more wine.

"I stepped through the memories of my mother, my aunt Catherine, of when we were in college. I thought about my sons and it just hit me. I realized these things were over. My life was over. I thought about Edna in *The Awakening* and her letting the ocean consume her. And I did just that. I walked into the surf and let the water overtake me."

"Oh my God, Lucy!" Eve said.

"The last thing I saw was the house before a wave pushed me to the bottom. I was drowning, and I realized that this is a place of my own. For me to become who I truly am, I needed to rebuild this place for me. I just barely made it back to shore."

"So, what happened next?" Diana asked.

"I had to break a window to get into the house, and I cleaned myself up and changed into some of my mother's clothes. Then I slept."

Lucy sipped her wine.

"The next morning I drove back into town. I'd left my keys in the car, but my phone was in my purse. That's why I never called. When I got back to the house, the gardeners were there and I paid them to pull everything out of the house, except for pictures of my boys, and put it all on the sidewalk. I made a sign, 'All Items One Dollar—Limit Ten Items.' I sold the entire contents of the house in less than three hours, and I mean everything. Theodore's clothes, his golf clubs and hunting rifles, antique furniture, paintings, and even the drapes. I made twelve hundred and eighty-three dollars and put it all in an envelope with Theodore's name on it and left it on the mantel."

"Damn, Lucy, and what did Theodore do?" Diana asked.

"As soon as he landed on his sister's dime, he was greeted at the airport and served with divorce papers. I'm sure he used that cash from the yard sale to find himself a room, because I cut off the power and telephone and put the house up for sale. Rather than ruin his precious reputation and job, he of course complied, hired an attorney, and quietly flew back to Paris."

"What about Teddy and William?" Eve asked.

"Both are very disappointed with their bigamist father. One of the hardest things about all of this was when I told them about what happened. Unlike their father, they are good young men and they came down and helped me clear this place out in time for the contractor. It took him just over a week to do the work. Funny how fast a contractor can move when you pay them extra. We moved the furniture in yesterday."

Lucy finished her wine and put the glass down. "I have something to show you." She reached for the silver box on the table. "This was my aunt Catherine's. It's an old cigarette box."

Lucy pulled the lid off, revealing a row of cigarettes.

"I remember she and my mother would sit at that old table on the back deck and they would have this out and sit and smoke cigarettes. A few days ago I realized the box has a false bottom."

Lucy pushed down on the bottom and it tilted up just enough to grab and lift out. Below it was a neat row of joints.

"Needless to say, I now realize why my mother loved having Aunt Catherine around."

Diana had to laugh and Eve had to think about it before realizing why it was funny.

Lucy stood up from her chair and picked up her glass and the silver cigarette case, and she gestured toward the back of the house. "Anyone for a waltz on the back porch?"

Eve and Diana both said yes and they grabbed their glasses of wine. A knock on the front door stopped them short.

"I wonder who that could be," Lucy said.

She put the silver box on the kitchen counter and unlocked the door. It was a man in his forties. His hair was a mottled mixture of blond and gray, and his skin was a rugged brown from years spent outdoors. He was wearing a pair of Levi's, and a white T-shirt under a blue unbuttoned short-sleeved shirt.

"Hey, I wanted to introduce myself," he said. "My name is…"

Pausing for a moment, he looked at Lucy in the most curious manner, a familiar way, and smiled at her, raising his eyebrows to ask a question.

"Hey, don't I know you?" he asked.

Lucy immediately knew who he was. It was their mysterious neighbor from the first summer she and the girls had vacationed at the beach house, but she acted as though she did not know him. "What's your name?" Lucy asked.

"Harrison."

"Yes, I do remember you from back when I was in college. You rented the place next door."

"That's right, I knew it. I remember your eyes most of all, and—" He stopped short and said, "I just bought the place from Mr. Taylor's son-in-law and wanted to meet my neighbors."

Harrison turned and pointed to a young girl on the back of his motorcycle. She was about nine years old and wearing a pink Hello Kitty helmet.

"That's my daughter, Violet. We used to live down in Beaufort, but after her mother passed away last year, I sold my bookstore and house and we've been traveling a lot, and when I heard Mr. Taylor passed away, I jumped at the chance to buy the place."

Harrison thrust his arm out and Lucy shook his hand.

"Hello, neighbor," he said.

"Well, hi there, neighbor," Lucy said.

Lucy waved to Violet, said good-bye to Harrison, and closed the door.

"Come on, girls, let's go waltzing in Vienna."

THE END

ABOUT THE AUTHOR

Born and raised in Columbia, South Carolina CG Metts charged into the underground art scene with a camera in one hand and a guitar in the other, and has never been quite the same. After earning Bachelor degrees in US History and Media Arts, Metts earned a Master's degree in film production from USC and has worked on numerous commercials, documentaries, and feature films. As a writer, Metts has written and published four non-fiction books including *Grave Words, Epitaphs of South Carolina* and *The Great Sea Islands Hurricane & Tidal Wave*. *WALTZING in VIENNA* is CG Metts' debut novel.

WALTZING in VIENNA

www.ingramcontent.com/pod-product-compliance
Lightning Source LLC
Chambersburg PA
CBHW020245180626
46810CB00006B/2381